She glanced away, a rosiness creeping into her cheeks.

"I'm just in a funk. I've made a mess of my life."

"You have?"

Josh's voice interrupted whatever Eunice might have said when he shouted, "Are you guys even looking?"

"He's hiding behind the water trough," Eunice said. "You want to find him this time, or should I?"

"How about we do it together?"

"Deal."

"And then we'll get dessert."

"Dessert does make most situations look better."

"Never makes things look worse."

But as they ambled over to the trough, where he could see his son's straw hat peeking out from the corner, Zeb couldn't help wondering why Eunice thought she'd made a mess of her life. As far as he could see, she'd made some pretty good choices. Never falling in love might not have its drawbacks— at least he assumed she'd never fallen in love. She'd never mentioned anyone that she cared about.

He admired that.

If you never put your heart out there, then it ~~couldn't~~ get broken...

Vannetta Chapman has published over one hundred articles in Christian family magazines and received over two dozen awards from Romance Writers of America chapter groups. She discovered her love for the Amish while researching her grandfather's birthplace of Albion, Pennsylvania. Her first novel, *A Simple Amish Christmas*, quickly became a bestseller. Chapman lives in Texas Hill Country with her husband.

Visit the Author Profile page at LoveInspired.com for more titles.

A Courtship for the Amish Spinster

VANNETTA CHAPMAN

LOVE INSPIRED
INSPIRATIONAL ROMANCE

LOVE INSPIRED®
INSPIRATIONAL ROMANCE

ISBN-13: 978-1-335-93682-0

A Courtship for the Amish Spinster

Love Inspired
22 Adelaide St. West, 41st Floor
Toronto, Ontario M5H 4E3, Canada
www.LoveInspired.com

Printed in Lithuania

MIX
Paper | Supporting responsible forestry
FSC® C021394

Children are an heritage of the Lord.
—*Psalm* 127:3

This book is dedicated to my students

Chapter One

Eunice Yoder stepped out of the barn and into a fine September evening. Northern Indiana in the fall was a *wunderbaar* place to be, and Shipshewana was the perfect little town. It was a good day, made better by the fact that Eunice had figured out what was wrong with the solar pump she'd been working on for her *bruder*-in-law Gideon. She had a little bounce in her steps and was looking forward to a nice dinner. Perhaps she'd even have a free hour to finish the novel she'd borrowed from the library the week before.

She was so pleased with herself and so busy planning her evening that she almost walked by Sarah's buggy without paying any attention to it. Honey nickered though, pulling Eunice's attention into the present. The chestnut mare had a rich brownish red coat. She was even-tempered and didn't mind waiting. Eunice thought Honey was a fine horse.

"Hey, girl. Didn't expect to see you tonight." Luckily she had a peppermint in her pocket for just such emergencies. Eunice unwrapped the candy, held it in her palm and waited for Honey to accept the gift. She didn't have to wait long.

Scratching the mare's neck, she whispered, "Guess I'll go see what my big sis is up to."

No one was on the porch, where they should have been on such a beautiful afternoon. No one was in the sitting room, which would have made some sense as they often visited there. She turned toward the kitchen, the first bells of alarm going off, and stopped in the doorway.

Her *dat* and *schweschder* sat at the table, patiently waiting for her by the looks on their faces. Sarah was taller than Eunice by a good four inches and rail thin. She was the oldest of the siblings and looked good. She looked content. Their *dat* had recently turned sixty years old, was somewhat round but not fat, and his hair and beard were quickly turning more gray than brown.

"Might as well come on in," Sarah said, patting the seat beside her.

"Not sure I want to."

"And yet, we need to speak to you." Her *dat* met her gaze and smiled softly. It didn't reach his eyes though, which was rare. Her father was usually in a jovial mood. Not this afternoon, not as he sat there studying her with something between concern and exasperation.

This looked serious.

Yikes.

She couldn't think of a single thing she'd done to embarrass her family or step outside the *Ordnung*. She breathed a sigh of relief that at least Bishop Ezekiel wasn't in attendance. So, it couldn't be terrible news. Ezekiel was like their long-lost uncle as well as their spiritual advisor. If something big was going down, Ezekiel would have been there.

"I brought dinner," Sarah said. "It's heating in the oven."

"Danki." Everyone knew that Eunice wasn't the best cook of the family, but they were getting by—her and her *dat*. Since Sarah had married and moved away, Eunice had been forced to learn the most basic of cooking skills. She thought she'd been doing okay. Was this about that?

Her father didn't waste any time. "We need to talk to you, Eunice. About your future."

"My future?"

Sarah chimed in with, "*Dat*'s worried, and so am I. We all are."

"You've been talking about my future to…everyone?"

"Not everyone," her *dat* corrected. "Your *schweschdern*, of course. Gideon, Aaron, Ethan and Noah all felt very strongly that it wasn't their place to voice an opinion."

Worse and worse.

If her four *bruders*-in-law were taking a hands-off approach, it must be very serious indeed.

She sat in the chair Sarah had gestured toward and crossed her arms. Then she uncrossed her arms because it felt very defensive to sit that way. She didn't want to appear defensive. This little meeting had all the signs of being bad enough.

"Okay. What am I in trouble for this time?"

"This time?" Sarah shook her head in mock surprise. "You act as if you stay in trouble."

"Well, last spring I was *taking unnecessary risks*." She emphasized the last three words and focused on not rolling her eyes. "Or so you all decided."

Sarah tsked. When had her oldest *schweschder* started tsking? "You were lying on the roof of a two-story house, hanging over the edge, trying to attach a solar panel."

"Actually the panel was already mounted on the roof of the house. I was dropping the wiring from the panel to the charging battery so that…" Eunice clamped her mouth shut. It was no use defending her activities that particular afternoon. Her *dat* had claimed it had taken a year off his life. What should have been a small, relatively easy job had earned her a scolding from all four *schweschdern*. "You know what. Never mind. Let's just get on with this. Whatever *this* is."

Instead of being offended by her abrupt manner, her *dat* nodded as if he was hoping she would see it that way. He opened his mouth to speak, shut it, patted the table and tried again. "Excellent. After speaking with your *schweschdern*, we are all concerned that you're not planning for your future."

Eunice let her head fall back and stared at the kitchen ceiling. She tried counting to ten, but then she noticed a spot on the ceiling that needed to be cleaned or painted. The five grandchildren in the Yoder family could make for a rambunctious bunch. There was no telling which one had decided to fling oatmeal up on the ceiling. Probably it was from a food fight gone awry. Not that they often had food fights, but five children were a lot to watch every second.

Yes, it had happened when she'd been left to watch over all the children. Her *schweschdern* had gone to clean house for one of the older men in their congregation who'd recently broken his hip. Eunice had told herself that she'd fetch the ladder and clean the ceiling before anyone noticed—yet there it remained, still on the ceiling, mocking her.

"Do you disagree?" Sarah asked.

"About what?"

Sarah and her *dat* shared a look, which caused Eunice to sit up straight and assume a serious demeanor. What had they been talking about? *Her future.* That was it. "I just don't know what you want from me. I'm working. I'm helping around the house."

"You're not dating." Her *dat* said this so softly that it made Eunice almost feel sorry for the man. He'd managed to successfully match all four of her *schweschdern*. He'd had no such luck with her, and she knew from previous conversations that he counted that as a personal failure.

"True. I'm not." Now she did cross her arms.

"Look, Eunice." Sarah cocked her head and waited.

She had the older-sister-but-kinda-your-mom thing down perfectly, probably because she had been Eunice's mom since Eunice was four years old. Since their *mamm* had died.

"You just turned twenty-five," Sarah continued.

"And you were thirty when you married."

"I'm not the best example."

"What is wrong with my being single?"

"I thought you might say that." Her *dat* actually looked relieved, as if finally the conversation was on the right track. "And we both know that my matchmaking attempts have been something of a flop. My fault, I fear. Not yours."

"Well, the last guy lived in Middlebury and had seven children. Seven, *Dat*. Do you really think I'm old enough and mature enough to instantly become the mother of seven?"

"I think you're old enough and mature enough to be anything you want to be, but…" And now he did look a bit lost. A bit older. A bit sad. "I'm afraid that you are too comfortable here. That it's easier to stay tinkering in the barn than it is to consider life beyond this farm."

"Becca didn't go beyond this farm. You can see her front porch from the kitchen window."

"And yet, she's married with a husband and two children. She is living her life. Her best life. And it's time for you to do the same."

Sarah jumped in before Eunice had the chance to respond to that, which was probably for the better. "There are parameters."

"Parameters? To what?"

"To the deal we're suggesting."

"You're suggesting a deal?"

"Either you find full-time employment, or you begin a serious courtship."

Huh. She could probably find a full-time job. It was September and shops would soon be hiring seasonal help as they extended their hours for Christmas shoppers. She didn't want to work in a shop, but she thought she could handle it long enough to calm everyone down. Someone would have a baby, the whole family would be distracted by the arrival and the attention would be off her.

"Okay. I don't think it's fair. I feel like I'm being pushed around, but I know you all mean well." She was actually starting to feel a bit nauseated and light-headed. If she'd known she was going to have to deal with this confrontation, she would have stayed in the barn. Which would only reinforce their point, so she didn't bring it up.

"You have thirty days," her father said.

"Thirty days?" The words came out louder, sharper than she intended.

"You keep kicking this particular can down the road, Eunice. I won't have it." Amos rarely took a stern voice with them. When he did, it was effective. "I will not have you hiding away in that barn, living like a spinster when you are only twenty-five years old."

"But…" Her brain picked that moment to betray her. She needed to say something, come up with some cogent argument, but her mind was suddenly and completely blank. Finally, she managed, "And if I don't?"

Her *dat* had already attempted to set her up with every eligible man in their church district and beyond; hence, the widowed guy in Middlebury with four girls and three boys. Whew. She wasn't that fond of children. Her nieces and nephews were great, of course. But seven kids of her own? No thanks.

"If you don't find full-time employment or begin dating seriously, then you'll be moving to Kentucky. I've already spoken with your cousins there."

"What?" She stood so abruptly, she nearly knocked the chair over. "Kentucky? You're sending me to Kentucky?"

"In thirty days, if you haven't—"

"Found full-time employment or begun a serious courtship. Heard you the first and the second time. But thirty days…"

"Should be plenty of time. Well. That's all settled." Sarah stood and began bustling around the kitchen. "Who wants cookies before dinner? I have oatmeal raisin, fresh from the oven."

But Eunice didn't want cookies. She didn't want dinner, and she didn't want to be in this room any longer. She excused herself and walked back out to the barn. The smell of linseed oil and hay and horse helped to ease her anxiety. This place, this barn, was where she was most comfortable, and she was good at what she did here. People from all over the area brought her their small engine machines. Yes, Amish had them. Their community was probably a bit on the liberal side of things in that regard, and it seemed that she'd always had this innate, mechanical ability.

Find full-time employment or begin a serious courtship.

She didn't want to spend her days looking for a job she wouldn't enjoy or be good at. And she knew absolutely no one that she'd be interested in dating.

Thirty days.

Or Kentucky.

Things were definitely worse than she'd thought.

She'd always loved working on broken things—taking them apart, figuring out what was wrong, devising a plan to fix them. But today she sat at the workbench and stared out the open door of the barn, wondering how she could fix what was wrong with her life. Wondering where she'd even start.

Chapter Two

Twenty-eight days later

Eunice walked out from the barn, wiping her hands on a greasy rag. She'd been working on a windmill's gearbox, and she must have been completely focused because she hadn't heard anyone drive up. Which explained why she was surprised to see Zebedee Mast and her father standing on their front porch.

As she walked toward them, Zeb shook hands with her father, then turned to jog down the porch steps.

"Zeb."

"Hey, Eunice."

Her *dat* turned to go inside, but Eunice caught the beginnings of a smile as he turned away. Now what was he up to? She knew that smile, and it usually foreshadowed one of his matchmaking schemes. But he'd given up on matchmaking. Hadn't he? He'd already purchased her bus ticket for Kentucky.

She was moving to Kentucky.

Glumly, she turned her attention back to Zeb. "Guess I didn't hear you drive up."

"About ten minutes ago. I wanted to drop off some papers with Amos."

"Papers?"

"Ya." He nodded as if that single word explained everything and continued on to his buggy.

Eunice hurried after him. "What kind of papers?"

"Oh, employment."

He attempted a smile, but to Eunice it looked more like something someone would paint on a scarecrow.

"Employment?" She forced her voice down. "You're going to work at the market?" Her father owned the Shipshewana Outdoor Market—the largest outdoor market in the Midwest. He employed a lot of local people—both Amish and *Englisch*. But Zeb?

"I am."

"But…why?"

His cheery bravado fell away, and he slumped against the side of the buggy. "Need the money, honestly. I guess you haven't heard. My folks are selling the farm."

"What?"

"I know. Still sounds bizarre to me, like a dream, or rather a nightmare. They're moving pretty soon actually."

"Where are they going?"

"Virginia."

"Why are so many old people moving? We've had at least three elderly couples move to Sarasota in the last year. What's the big deal with Florida?"

"I don't know about Sarasota, but Virginia was on the list the doctor gave to *Mamm*."

"There was a list?"

"California."

"Not many Amish there."

"Hawaii."

They both laughed.

"Colorado and Virginia."

"I heard there's a small community in Colorado. A town called Monte Vista."

"Yup. There are three there in total—Westcliffe, La Jara and Monte Vista."

"But your parents didn't choose Colorado."

"Nope. *Mamm*'s *schweschder*, my *aenti*, lives in Virginia. So that's where they picked. It's a big change, but *Mamm* says her arthritis hurts all the time here in Indiana, and *Dat*…" Zeb sighed. "He just wants to make *Mamm* happy."

"I'm sorry, Zeb. I didn't know."

"My *bruder* and I are trying to come up with enough money for a down payment."

"You need a down payment?" Eunice was trying to catch up, but this was a lot to take in at once. Beneath her questions for Zeb ran the constant refrain she'd struggled with the last twenty-eight days. *Why did things have to change?*

"It will have to be a proper sale as my parents need the money for a new, smaller place in Virginia. I was hoping being employed at your *dat*'s market would bolster my bid on the place. You know, the bank has to consider whether you're a *gut* risk or not. But what I really need is more cash, and that will take a few months of working. In the meantime, if another buyer submits a contract first…"

"Oh." Eunice didn't spend much time thinking about money. Okay, she never thought about it. She was twenty-five years old and lived with her father. Soon she'd be twenty-five years old and living with her *aenti*. Either way, money wasn't exactly an issue.

Zeb's situation was different.

Zeb was her age, but he was already a widower. His wife had died of cancer. Now he was raising his five-year-old son alone. "What will you do with Josh while you're working?"

"Honestly, I don't know. Sorta taking it one step at a time.

I wanted to be sure I had a job first, before I looked for child-care."

"Amish don't really do childcare. Usually family helps."

"My only family is my *bruder*." Zeb shrugged. "I can't imagine Samuel watching after Josh."

"I can't either." Eunice thought Samuel was a nice guy but rather distracted. He was always losing his bike or forgetting where he parked the family buggy or leaving his hat somewhere. The fact that he was older than Zeb, older than Eunice, and still rode a bike rather than owning a horse and buggy spoke to the fact that he wasn't exactly mature, nephew-watching material.

"Could be worse," Eunice said. "Your family could be shipping you off to Kentucky."

"Still no beau?"

She glowered at him, and he held his hands up—palms out. "Didn't mean that the way it sounded. Sorry."

"No beau. No full-time job."

Zeb was five-foot-ten with a thin build and unruly, brown hair. In fact, his hair reminded Eunice of Bethany's son, Daniel. The boy had a real mop of curls even though he was only seven months old. Zeb's deep blue eyes often seemed troubled, like they were now. Zeb was usually worried about something. She supposed life had taught him to be on guard against the unexpected.

"What will you be doing at the market?" Eunice asked.

He attempted a smile which looked sort of pathetic. Weren't they just the pair. Anyone walking by would think that someone had died.

"I'll be the Amish-*Englisch* liaison."

"Liaison?" Eunice started laughing. She couldn't help it. Zeb's offended look only made her laugh harder.

"What's so funny?"

"Nothing. It just sounds—well, it sounds more *Englisch* than Amish."

"I guess."

"What will you do?"

"Amos wants to start behind-the-scene tours at the market."

"Ah. Very mysterious happenings there, for sure and certain. That should be a real hit. They can see how to clean out a horse stall, milk a cow or run a cotton candy machine."

"Go ahead and make fun." And now the beginnings of a real smile softened his features. "Amos started advertising last week, and he already has had a lot of interest. He's been holding off selling tickets until we could work out my hours. I think the tours are going to be popular."

"Seriously?"

"Yup. I'm about to be a very busy tour guide."

"How do you feel about that? Leading tour groups around isn't exactly the quintessential Amish job."

"I love when you use big words like that."

"Whatever. You used *liaison*." She bumped her shoulder against his.

They'd always been like that—best of friends in school, competing with one another, hanging out together. Other girls didn't seem to know what to do with Eunice. She was too mechanically minded and definitely not interested in quilting or baking. As for other boys, they'd kept a wide berth as if she might have a contagious disease. Only Zeb had accepted her for who she was—a not-so-Amish Amish girl.

When he'd married and moved away, she'd lost her best friend. When he'd moved back to Shipshe, he was different—hurt and angry and introverted. This was the most she'd seen him smile in a while. Maybe the job at the market would be good for him.

"I'm sure you'll be a great tour guide." She nodded toward the barn. "I'm working on Ezekiel's windmill. Guess I better get back to it."

She didn't go back into the barn though. As Zeb drove away, she remembered the expression on her *dat*'s face. She'd need to address that, and the sooner the better. It was probably time for dinner anyway. She'd need to forage around in the refrigerator and come up with something.

If it weren't for her *schweschder* Becca making twice what her family needed, they'd be stuck eating sandwiches. Cooking had never been a part of Eunice's skill set, though she'd spent much of one summer trying to learn how to meal plan, prep and cook. Ha. That had resulted in a lot of terrible-tasting food. Finally, her oldest *schweschder*, Sarah, had shooed her off to the barn, and Eunice had resumed doing what she was good at—fixing broken things.

Sarah was married now. All of her *schweschdern* were married.

Eunice and her *dat* had been making the best of an unusual situation—a widowed father and one remaining, unwed *doschder* who couldn't cook. She thought there might be some chicken casserole left over that they could reheat for dinner.

Her *dat* was sitting at the kitchen table, paperwork spread around him. Eunice sat down across from him and waited for him to look up.

"How was your day?" he asked.

"*Gut.* And yours?"

"*Gut.*"

He waited. She waited.

Finally he tidied the papers and stuck them into a folder. "Did you want to talk about something?"

"*Ya*, I do."

Now his smile broadened, causing the skin around his eyes to crinkle, and Eunice had to work to hold on to her aggravation.

She leaned forward and lowered her voice. "I know what you're doing."

"You do?"

Instead of answering that question, she began ticking names off on her fingertips. "Gideon. Aaron. Ethan. Noah."

"All wonderful men—and employees. Though technically, Ethan isn't employed by me anymore. Only when he has extra time on his hands and can—"

"It won't work, *Dat*."

"What won't work?"

"Setting me up with Zeb. How could you? Zeb and I are best friends. At least, we were best friends before he married and moved away."

"You're not still friends?"

"Of course we are, but Zeb is different now."

Amos nodded and his expression grew quite serious. "Grief is a difficult thing. Zeb needs time, and he also needs a job. It's the least I can do to help the young man."

"A tour guide?"

"I've been thinking of starting tours for some time."

"Uh-huh."

"If you're thinking that I'm matchmaking, maybe you're projecting your own hopes onto me."

"I am not."

"So you're not interested in Zeb romantically?"

"You need to listen to me, *Dat*. Zeb is my friend. One of my only friends."

"That's not true. You have plenty of friends."

"No, I have acquaintances." She let out a frustrated sigh.

"I'm okay with that. I'm like a round peg in a land of square holes."

"I don't know what that means."

"It means that I don't plan to lose Zeb's friendship by indulging schoolgirl daydreams."

"You had daydreams about him?" The smile was back.

"I do believe that you are incorrigible. In case you've forgotten, you already purchased my bus ticket. I leave in two days. Admit it—you failed in finding me the perfect man. So off to Kentucky I go."

Amos held up his hands in surrender. "I understand that you're not excited about the move, but we had a deal. You had—"

"Thirty days, I know."

"Which means you have—"

"Two left." Hmm. Maybe a beau would fall out of the sky. Or a job offer would appear in their mailbox. She'd had no luck looking for a full-time job. Lots of part-time stuff out there, but nothing that she could claim would support herself if need be.

"It's true that I worry about you. I'm not going to live forever you know." And like a wind that swept across the fields, his smile fell away and that familiar look of worry crept into his eyes.

It was a look she couldn't resist.

A look that she and Sarah, Bethany and Becca, even Ada had seen too often. Eunice remembered precious little about her mother since she had been four when her *mamm* had died from cancer, but she was well aware that her father was a very special person. He had always been there for her, had shouldered the duties of two parents, had kept his five daughters' best interests at heart.

Maybe that also explained why she couldn't be angry with

him about this forced move. He really thought it was best for her. How did you fault someone for loving you?

She stood, walked around the table and kissed him on the cheek. "*Danki*. But there is nothing for you to worry about."

Eunice understood that her *dat* cared for her very much. She also knew that her marrying prospects were nonexistent. She had come to terms with that, and one way or the other, he would have to come to terms with it too. Moving to Kentucky wasn't likely to change a thing.

Zeb was unharnessing Beauty—a dapple gray mare with one white sock—when Joshua dashed into the barn. His son was five years old, small for his age and the joy of his heart.

"*Dat!*" Josh wrapped his arms around Zeb's legs. "Where did you go without me?"

"Business." He tussled Josh's blond hair—a shade that reminded him of the boy's mother, Suzanne.

"What kind of business?" Josh walked over to Beauty and proceeded to scratch the mare's neck.

Zeb handed him a grooming brush. Josh grinned as if he'd been given a new toy, found his stool, pulled it over next to the horse and began brushing in short, gentle strokes.

"I accepted a job today," Zeb explained. "That's where I went. To tell the man—to tell Amos Yoder—that I had agreed to take the job. I'm going to be working at the market. You went there with me last weekend. Remember?"

"Sure."

"The job Amos offered me will be a *gut* one."

"So you'll be gone during the day?"

"I will—only three days a week at first."

"Okay. Can I go with you?"

"*Nein*. You'll stay…"

"With *Mammi*?"

"For the first few weeks." Actually he wasn't sure of his parents' exact move date. They had talked to a real estate agent in Halifax County, and the agent had found them a rental. It would do for the first few months. Until they had the profit from the sale of the farm.

"Next year I'll go to school."

"Yes, you will."

"Okay." He clamored off the stool and walked over to his father, held up his right hand for Zeb to slap.

It was all Zeb could do not to laugh at the *Englisch* gesture and the serious expression on his son's face. He high-fived his little boy.

"Deal then," Josh said. "You'll go to work, and I'll help *Mammi*."

"Deal."

Then Josh said the words that landed like an arrow in the center of Zeb's heart. "Do you think *Mamm* would have liked Beauty?"

"Ya."

"I do too." He reached up to wrap his arms around the horse's neck and remarkably Beauty put her head down as if to make it easier on the child. "*Mammi*'s baking cookies. I better go see if I can help."

"Put the brush and stool up first."

"Right." He put the brush in a small cubby, then ran back and snagged the stool, placing it next to the cubby, then ran out of the barn.

His son was at the age where he ran everywhere. It didn't matter if he was going a dozen steps away or a hundred. He literally dashed from here to there, there to here. His energy was something that always amazed Zeb.

Do you think Mamm *would have liked Beauty?*

Josh mentioned his mother at least once a day, often more

than that. Immediately after Suzanne's death it had been once an hour. Zeb had spoken to his parents about it, and they had suggested he speak with Ezekiel. He'd called his old bishop from the phone booth near his home in Lancaster, Pennsylvania. That's where he'd lived with Suzanne. Where Josh had been born. Where Suzanne was buried.

Ezekiel had been a guiding force throughout Zeb's young adulthood. He had even married Zeb and Suzanne, and he'd traveled the six hundred miles with Zeb's family to attend Suzanne's funeral. It was the bishop who had given Zeb the best advice regarding his young son. "He's processing what he's lost. Give him the space and time to do that."

He would.

He absolutely would.

Josh had been three years old when his *mamm* had died from uterine cancer. At first, Zeb was too deep in his own grief to understand how it had affected his little boy. He understood that some crying was normal. He'd cried a good bit in those first few days himself. Then the grief had settled like a stone in his soul, and he'd stopped crying.

Josh had taken longer to recover. He'd lost interest in playing, in eating, in everything. It had been frightening to see his son hurting and not know how to help him.

He's processing what he's lost. Give him the space and time to do that.

It was one of the reasons he'd moved back to Shipshewana. He'd hoped the change in location would help his young son recover. The good news was that Josh had become interested in life again, but he still mentioned his *mamm* every day.

Zeb could relate to a little of what his son must be experiencing. He hadn't lost his mother, but he'd lost the woman that he'd planned to spend the rest of his life with. He was very sure that if he were given all the space in northern Indiana and all the time in the world, it wouldn't help him process what they had both lost.

It was still completely unfathomable to him.

How had his life gone so terribly wrong? How had tragedy found him? And how was he supposed to move forward when his heart was still very much in Lancaster?

He didn't think being an Amish tour guide would help in that regard. But it would provide some much-needed income. He was grateful that Amos had offered him the job. Quick on the heels of that offer was Eunice's reaction to the news. Did she not think he'd make a good tour guide? Did she think he'd be a terrible employee? Did she think he should be home with his son?

Eunice Yoder was a mystery to him.

She was unlike any woman he'd ever met.

He wasn't a bit surprised that she hadn't married yet. Eunice managed to intimidate most men simply by her reputation. She could fix any mechanical device found on an Amish farm and a few that weren't. She must want more than that though. Surely she planned to marry one day, to have a husband and children.

"Not my business," he murmured under his breath.

He had plenty of problems of his own. He didn't need to borrow someone else's.

Zeb's *bruder*, Samuel, walked into the barn at that moment.

"You're home from the market early," Zeb said.

His brother was three years older, worked on both the auction side of Amos's market and the RV side. Then, if he had any time left at all—which he usually didn't—he helped around the farm.

"It's nearly five." Samuel plopped onto the stool next to

the workbench. "I wasn't about to miss one of *Mamm*'s last meals."

"Don't remind me."

Samuel shrugged, a gesture that only served to irritate Zeb more. "Not much we can do about it, *bruder*. They're moving. Might as well accept it. *Mamm* has boxes stacked all over the house. We'll be lucky if they leave us a can opener."

"Why this sudden desire to up and move and just…just leave us? Don't you find it all a bit strange?"

"Not really. Lots of Amish retire to places where the winter isn't so harsh."

"But we're here. Josh is here."

"And I'm sure they love us and Josh very much. But you've seen *Mamm*'s hands in the morning. Cramped up so tightly that she can barely hold a coffee cup. I say, if the warmer weather stands any chance of helping her arthritis, they should go."

"You're right."

"I usually am."

Zeb glowered at him, and Samuel laughed. "I didn't create this situation. I'm just reminding you of the facts."

"Thanks for that."

"How did it go with Amos?"

"Fine."

"So you'll start in a couple days?"

"I'll help around the auction until the first tour which is on the sixteenth."

"Huh." Samuel took his hat off, slapped it against the workbench.

"What?"

"What do you mean *what*?"

"You didn't come out here to chat with me about *Mamm*'s packing."

"True enough. Have you found a sitter for Josh yet?"

"Nope."

"*Mamm* wants you to consider Tabitha. Says she's a sweet girl, and she's already minding two other children. So Josh will have kids to play with."

"Not going to happen."

"Because?"

"Because Tabitha is only sixteen. She's a kid herself."

"*Mamm*'s worried that you're ignoring the problem."

Zeb had been tidying the area where they groomed the horses. Now he sank back against the barn wall and let his head fall into his hands.

"I'm not ignoring the problem. I don't know anyone here that well, not well enough to trust them with Josh."

"You grew up here."

"I did, but Shipshe has changed. People have moved in, moved out, married, become widowed. I don't know who would want to help me out, and before you start naming women, don't. They're either too young, or they'd see it as an overture of sorts."

"Overture?"

"They'd think I'm interested."

"What's wrong with that?"

"I'm not interested."

Samuel stared up at the ceiling for a minute, then finally blew out a big breath. "I get that. I'm three years older, and I'm not ready to settle down."

Zeb rolled his eyes. To Samuel, the world was a playground. Of course he wasn't ready to settle down. That wasn't exactly a news flash.

Samuel snapped his fingers. "I've got it. What about Eunice?"

"Eunice who?"

"Eunice Yoder, your boss's *doschder*."

"Oh. Yeah. I know who Eunice is."

"So. What about her? I heard that Amos is sending her to Kentucky because she won't marry or find a full-time job."

That wasn't exactly correct. Amos wasn't insisting that she marry. He was insisting that she get serious about the next phase of her life. Zeb didn't want to explain the distinction to Samuel though.

What was it Eunice had said to him earlier?

No beau. No full-time job.

He didn't put his nose in other people's business, which meant he didn't know the particulars of Eunice's situation. Only that if she didn't get serious about growing up, her *dat* was going to insist she move. In fact, word was he'd already bought the bus ticket. Eunice was grown up, in Zeb's opinion. She was just different. She was... Eunice.

Samuel dusted imaginary dust off the workbench, his eyes pinned on Zeb. "Well?"

"Well what?"

"Well, what do you think about asking Eunice?"

"I'm not sure that will work."

"But it might."

Instead of answering, Zeb tried to picture Eunice with a small child. He shook his head. "Can't see it. You know Eunice."

"Barely."

"She's good with machines...with windmills and solar panels and pumps."

"Maybe Josh could help her with her work."

"He's five." Zeb held up his right hand, fingers splayed, as if Samuel needed help understanding the number five. "What if he got hurt?"

"That wouldn't happen."

"It might. She just doesn't seem like the motherly type."

"But you're not looking for a mother. You're looking for a sitter." When Zeb didn't respond to that, Samuel stood and stretched. "Chicken casserole and fresh-baked bread for dinner. Don't be late or there might not be any left." Then he walked out of the barn.

Leaving Zeb to puzzle over the idea of Eunice Yoder watching his son.

It might work. It was possible that they could solve each other's problem.

Eunice needed a full-time job, so she could stay in Shipshe. Zeb didn't need a full-time sitter. But if she found another part-time job, if she could schedule her hours when he wasn't doing tours...

It was possible that two part-time jobs would do the trick.

It was also true what he'd said to his *bruder*. Eunice did not seem like the motherly type.

But at least he knew her well.

He supposed he would feel okay leaving Josh in her care.

He sat down on the stool his *bruder* had been occupying and studied the pegboard full of tools above the workbench. *A place for everything and everything in its place.* That was a favorite saying of his *dat*'s.

Zeb strongly felt that his place—his and Josh's place—was here in Indiana. It wasn't back in Lancaster. There had been too many memories of Suzanne there. He'd felt immobilized by the constant reminders of her.

Here in Shipshe things were different. He could—for a few minutes every day—forget what he had lost.

Samuel didn't understand what it was like for him.

Samuel had lived in Shipshe all of his life.

Most Amish women were married and had plenty of children of their own. The ones that weren't...and there were a few in their church congregation, like Tabitha…were either young or searching for a man. He didn't like the idea of leaving his son with a teenager. A woman who was older than that and unmarried would see any such request as an overture. They would think he was romantically interested in them.

But Eunice would know it was business.

Just business.

That was how he'd present it to her. They were both in something of a pickle, but maybe they could help each other out. That's what friends did. Right? And they had been friends, a long time ago, when they were still in school.

Before Suzanne.

And the cancer.

And Josh.

He'd see her first thing in the morning. He'd see her before she boarded that bus. He was desperate and so was she. What could possibly go wrong?

A lot.

A lot of things could go wrong.

But he didn't have the luxury of indulging those thoughts. He needed to make a decision, and he needed to do so before his job started in two days. Though his *mamm* was happy to watch Josh for the immediate future, she was pretty consumed with boxing things up for the move. He'd talk to Eunice.

Then he'd pray that it wasn't a mistake.

Chapter Three

Eunice was surprised to hear the clatter of buggy wheels after her *dat* had left for the market. No one was bringing her a gadget to work on. She might as well nail an *Off to Kentucky* sign on the barn door for all the business she had. And she couldn't blame them. She was leaving for her *aenti*'s the next day.

The next day.

She wanted to put her head in her hands and weep. She wanted to storm into her father's office and argue that he couldn't make decisions about her life. She wanted to remind him that she was a grown woman. She didn't do any of those things mainly because this was a solution she'd agreed to. So instead, she walked out into an overcast October day to see who had come to visit.

"Zeb. Is everything okay?"

Zeb didn't do social visits. And she'd seen him the night before. She hurried toward his buggy thinking maybe he'd forgotten to leave an employment form with her *dat*.

"He isn't here right now, but if you have something for *Dat*, I can see that he gets it."

Zeb set the brake and hopped out of the buggy. He started to speak, stopped, stuck his hands in his pockets, then looked left and right.

"I can see the proverbial cat has your tongue. Want to sit on the porch?"

"Sure. That would be *gut*."

But once they were seated, he still seemed ill at ease. He'd plucked his straw hat off his head and held it in his hands. His gaze couldn't settle on any one thing. And his left leg was jiggling, which reminded Eunice of when they'd had tests in school. Zeb had always been a nervous tester.

"I'm here…" He cleared his throat.

She waited.

He tried again. "I'm here to ask you something. It made sense to me last night, and then this morning less so. By the time I pulled into your driveway, I was sure I'd made a mistake."

"Now I'm curious."

"The thing is that we both have a problem."

"We do?"

"Your *dat* wants you…well, I'm not sure what he wants."

Eunice wanted to melt into the porch floor from embarrassment. If it had been anyone other than Zeb, she would have changed the subject. But Zeb wasn't bringing this up due to mild curiosity or to feed the Amish grapevine. So, instead of being offended, she pulled in a deep breath and told him the truth.

"They think I'm hiding in the barn."

"They?"

"My *dat*, Sarah, Becca, Bethany, even Ada."

"Oh."

"They think that's why I haven't dated and why I don't have a job. Because I'm more comfortable hiding in the barn."

"Oh," he said again.

"They gave me thirty days, which ends tomorrow." She tried to smile brightly. It felt fake. It was fake. She gave up on that. "I'm twenty-five years old, and my family is shipping me off to Kentucky like some parcel they don't know what to do with."

He opened his mouth and Eunice said, "Do not say *oh* again."

"Right." Zeb cleared his throat. "So, as I was saying, I wanted to ask you something. Here goes."

Eunice had a queasy feeling in her stomach.

What was he so nervous about?

He was making her nervous.

"I want to ask if you'd consider watching Josh."

Eunice looked around. Was Josh with him? Had she somehow overlooked the child?

"On the days I work at the market, on the tours."

"Well. The first problem with that is that *I'm going to Kentucky*." She emphasized the last four words and drew them out slowly.

"But what if you didn't?"

"Not following."

"You said you needed a full-time job."

"Which I cannot find, and trust me I've looked."

"But what if you had two part-time jobs? Would that satisfy your *dat*'s requirement?"

"Hmm."

"So it might?"

"It might." Eunice set her chair to rocking. What he was suggesting was crazy. She knew next to nothing about taking care of five-year-old boys, but how hard could it be? If she could take a solar pump apart and put it back together, certainly she could handle one small boy. "I'm a little puzzled. Why me?"

Zeb looked as if he'd been caught, and she knew she'd hit the nail on the head with that question.

"Plenty of *youngies*, even women, would be willing to earn a little extra money. Why me, Zeb?"

He shifted uncomfortably in the chair, then seemed to accept that he might as well tell her. As usual, he began ticking items off on his fingers. "I don't want to leave Josh with a woman who has a house full of kids. He'd just be one more child. She might lose him."

"Doubtful, but go on."

"And I don't like the idea of a teenager watching him. I know that people say they're quite responsible, and I suppose some are. But it's not what I want for my son."

Eunice waited. There was at least one more reason. Zeb was still staring at his hand, ready to tick off point number three.

When he continued to hesitate, she leaned forward and said, "Just tell me."

"Okay. Some women—not you, but *some women*—would see this as an overture to a relationship. They would think that I was interested in dating. They'd think I was using Joshua as an excuse to check them out first."

"Trying them out for the mommy job?"

"Exactly. I knew you'd understand."

Eunice was pretty sure she did not understand.

"Trust me, I made that mistake in Lancaster. It did not end well. The young woman was crying, and I was trying to explain myself, and Josh had no idea what was happening." He shook his head, dropped his hands and clutched the rocker as if he was afraid he was about to be thrown out of it.

"Should I be offended?"

"What? No. Why would you ask that?"

"Because I'm not like them, not like some women, that I would never misinterpret your motive." She was half kidding and half serious. She was, after all, a flesh and blood woman who wouldn't mind thinking that a man was interested in her. The look on Zeb's face though, it was enough to push her away from the offended side of things. When she grinned at him, he let out a relieved sigh.

"See? That's what I mean. We've been friends forever. I knew you wouldn't take this the wrong way."

So, he still thought of her as his childhood friend. Well, wasn't that how she thought of him? Maybe, some days. Other days, when he was sitting on her porch, cleaned up and looking nice, she did wonder…

"It wouldn't be full-time, of course. Surely you could find another part-time job to go with it."

"Mrs. Lancaster did offer me a job at the yarn shop. I know next to nothing about yarn, but she offered to teach me. The position was for twenty hours a week."

"Do you think she'd be flexible regarding your schedule?"

"Probably not. She needs someone on Monday, Tuesday and Saturday."

"Okay." Zeb hopped up and began to pace. "That could work. We could schedule future tours on Wednesday, Thursday and Friday. Those are pretty busy days anyway. Lots of tourists about because they're taking off midweek, adding in a weekend, and ending up with five days of vacation. So, yeah. Wednesday, Thursday and Friday could work. As long as Amos agrees."

"I'm sure he would. Do you really think you'll have enough tourists on those days?"

"Samuel said as much about the RV park. Lots of folks come in on Wednesday, leave Sunday or Monday."

"When do your tours start?"

"Tomorrow, but my *mamm* is still here for a few days. I'd need you to start next week."

"Okay. I say we give it a try." Eunice smiled at him, even

though she was feeling a little uncertain about this change in plans. It wasn't like she had wanted to move to Kentucky, but this… Was she really going to keep Zeb's kid? Did he trust her to do that? "I've taken care of my nieces and nephews before. How hard can one boy be?"

"Suzanne's *schweschder* used to say that one was harder than four."

Eunice didn't know how to respond to that. Zeb rarely if ever brought up his wife or her family. It was like a part of his life that he didn't want to talk about, so she'd never pushed him on it. Instead of responding, she simply shrugged.

"You could always ask Becca for help, seeing as she lives so close and all."

"Sure, but I doubt I'll need to do that." Eunice was picturing the inside of a barn. It had been her domain for so long. Now she'd be away every day. "So I'd be working six days a week."

"Well. Yes. You would. But it would only be half days, right? So it isn't as if you'd be working eight hours a day for six days."

"True."

"Do you think your *dat* will go for this plan?"

"He might."

Zeb had walked to the porch steps and was staring out over their fields. Eunice joined him there, wondering what he was seeing. Wondering what he was thinking about. Zeb was quiet a lot of the time. He seemed…lost in his thoughts.

Finally, she cleared her throat and said, "Don't worry about Josh. I'm sure he and I will get along just fine."

"I can make you a list."

"A list?"

"A cheat sheet of sorts."

Eunice tried to hold in the laughter, because Zeb seemed

serious—very serious. He was always serious. But she couldn't keep her laughter from bubbling out.

He looked at her in surprise. "What?"

"Last time we tried a cheat sheet..."

Understanding dawned on his face. "Fifth grade. Math exam."

"We were caught and had to clean the board for two weeks solid."

"Plus I was grounded by my parents."

"My *dat* did the same."

Eunice thought that it was funny, remembering the children they'd been. How had they ended up here?

"Let's give it a try," Eunice said. "I'll speak to my *dat* this evening and let you know."

He nodded once, tightly. *"Danki."*

"Gem Gschehne." She said the words softly, and for a moment his expression became something kinder, something not filled with worry. The moment passed and his usual, troubled expression returned.

Slapping his hat on his head, he attempted a smile.

As he drove away, Eunice stood there watching his buggy until it was a spot at the far end of the lane. Zeb needed help with his child. She was glad he'd come to her. But there was more than that on his mind. Zeb Mast was not a happy guy. She couldn't blame him. Losing a wife had to be hard. But that had been over two years ago. Shouldn't he have moved on by now?

But then who was she to judge? She was still working in the barn. She had been tinkering on small machines since she was fourteen years old and let loose from the schoolhouse. Eleven years had passed. How? How had her life, her future, her dreams become so small?

Perhaps her *dat* was right. Maybe the barn, this farm, her family—maybe they had all provided a safe place to hide.

She wouldn't be hiding anymore.

A small part of her was actually looking forward to the change, but she most certainly did not think she'd need a cheat sheet to take care of one small boy. Another part of her understood that she wasn't exactly facing her problems. Caring for a friend's child and working for a yarn shop wasn't embracing her future or planning for the rest of her life.

It was a small step in the right direction though.

She had no idea if it would be enough—for her father or for herself.

But she planned to find out.

Zeb got word the next day from his *bruder*, who'd heard it from Gideon, who'd been told by Eunice that her *dat* had agreed to their plan. He supposed an *Englischer* would have simply texted "We're good to go," but they weren't *Englisch*, and no one that he knew owned a cell phone.

Correction. He'd seen some of the *youngies* in town with cell phones. Personally, he couldn't imagine setting aside money for such a thing. The message from Eunice to Gideon to Samuel to Zeb worked just fine.

Things in his life were changing quickly. He now had a babysitter for his son, a new job guiding *Englischers* on tours and his parents' relocation date had been moved up. Wow. When they decided something, they moved quickly. As his *mamm* had said the night before, "What's the point in dragging our feet?" Deborah Mast was no one's fool.

Zeb suspected she knew the longer they took to leave, the harder it would be.

He walked into the house to find even more chaos than when he'd walked out of the house at lunch. His *mamm* had pulled out everything from the kitchen cabinets and was putting a good portion of it in boxes. She was tackling the moving project like a woman twenty years younger. His *mamm* had kept in *gut* shape. She was fifty-seven, but she still seemed young to him. Except for her hands.

She smiled when he walked in. "Want some coffee?"

"I'll get it." Zeb turned in a circle. "Where's the coffee-pot?"

"Oh. Guess I packed it. What was I thinking? We'll need coffee the rest of the week." She began pawing through one box and then another.

"Don't worry about it, *Mamm*. Water's fine." He fetched a glass, filled it from the tap and sat down at the table next to Josh. "Whatcha drawing, son?"

"A horse." The horse in question had an enormous head and was taller than the house it stood beside. "I don't think I have his ears right though."

"Ears are hard," Zeb agreed. He drank half the glass, then turned to his *mamm*. "I just talked to Samuel."

"Your *bruder*'s home?"

"*Ya*, he's in the barn."

Josh popped out of his chair. "I need to show him my picture." He dashed out of the room, made it to the front door, looked down at his empty hands, dashed back into the kitchen, grabbed the drawing and took off.

"A lot of energy in that one," Deborah said.

"Indeed." Zeb cleared his throat, ready to get this portion of the evening over with. It wasn't that he thought his *mamm* wouldn't approve, but she had strong feelings regarding his personal life and Josh's. He guessed that was normal. "So, I think I have childcare worked out for Josh."

"Oh, honey. That's *wunderbaar*." Deborah stared down into a box, found and retrieved the percolator coffeepot and put it back on the stove. With a sigh, she walked to the table and sat down beside him. "Tell me all about it."

"Well, it was Samuel's idea, actually, that I ask Eunice Yoder."

Deborah clapped her hands. "Eunice. I've always liked her."

He explained about the arrangement Eunice had with her *dat*, the impending move to Kentucky and the plan they'd come up with to help one another out of a tight spot.

"That's what friends do," Deborah chirped. "I remember you and Eunice hanging out together when you were both in school. At one point I even thought you might be sweet on her."

Zeb laughed, though to him it sounded more like nervous laughter than anything genuine. His mind didn't want to go there. He supposed that he believed that the mere thought of being interested in someone else, even in the years before he'd met Suzanne, felt like a betrayal.

So instead of talking about who he might or might not have been sweet on, he clarified, "This isn't like that though. It's purely business."

"Business among friends."

"Exactly."

"Unless *Gotte* has something else in mind."

"Uh-uh. Nope. Don't start thinking that way, *Mamm*."

"Okay. I understand." She patted his hand, then winked. She most certainly did not understand, and they both knew it. Fortunately, she changed the subject. "I want you to know that I am aware how inconvenient this move is for you. I'm sorry that it's happening now. I'm sorry we can't be here for you and Josh and Samuel."

She stared down at her hands, and Zeb saw—maybe for the first time—just how misshapen her knuckles were. Of course, he'd known that his *mamm* suffered from rheumatoid arthritis for some time, but he hadn't really paid attention. He'd been too distracted by his own troubles.

Now he covered her hands with his, squeezing them very lightly. "It'll be *gut* for you to be near your *schweschder*. And the doctor said that Virginia would be a smart move. Mild winters, at least compared to what we have, and less humidity than the southern states."

"I suppose so. No clouds are so dark that God cannot see through them."

"Bible verse?"

"Amish proverb."

He thought that their conversation was over. He'd even pushed away from the table, but Deborah cocked her head and started to say something, then stopped, then started again. "Sometimes love looks different the second time around."

Not this again. He really didn't need this. He had enough on his mind without the *you should be dating again* lecture. And maybe if she'd met his gaze and wagged a finger his direction he would have just smiled and walked away.

But Deborah didn't do that.

She stared at her hands, rubbing the fingers of one over the swollen knuckles of the other.

"First love is exciting. It's nervous anticipation and long looks and nights tossing in bed wondering if you're imagining what you're feeling. I'm not saying it isn't real." She glanced up and smiled softly. "It's as real as this table or my swollen hands."

Zeb waited. He knew there was more. Best to hear her out now. She would have her say, and apparently the impending move was giving her motherly angst. As if she couldn't put her advice in a letter or speak it into a phone. As if she needed to say this face-to-face. He wasn't sure how he knew that, but he did. He'd learned to read people better since being married to Suzanne. He'd learned to give someone time to say what was in their heart.

"Second love though…well, of course we pray that it never comes to that. We hope and pray that the one we love in our youth will be by our side when we're old. It didn't happen that way for me. I was engaged to a very nice young man when I was only eighteen."

Zeb nearly fell out of his chair. Had she said she'd been engaged to another man? He hadn't heard this before. He knew that she was twenty-five when she'd married his father.

"He left the faith, or at least the Amish way. I couldn't say whether he still follows the teachings of Christ. I hope he does. We lost contact after he moved—to New York City if you can believe that."

"You've never mentioned this before."

"You didn't need to know then, but maybe…" She let her gaze drift around the kitchen and then finally land, softly land, on him. "Maybe you do now. I was hurt after that experience. Didn't believe I'd ever fall in love again. Certainly never thought I'd marry."

"And then you met *Dat*."

Her worried expression morphed into the tenderest of smiles. "Not right away. And even when I did meet him, it took time before I would even consider the idea of love. You see, Zeb, I'd been hurt by the man who left."

"He didn't leave *you*."

"Well. He left our Amish lifestyle—something I couldn't imagine doing. When he left our community, our way of life, he also left me, and that was painful."

"Wasn't your fault though."

"Of course it wasn't, just as Suzanne's leaving wasn't your fault."

He shook his head. "Different situation."

"It is. It most certainly is." She stood then, walked behind his chair and kissed him on the top of the head. It made him feel like a child. It made him feel loved and valued. "Just remember, son. Second love is different, but it's every bit as precious."

She kept talking, even as she once again pawed through a box of things she'd packed. "I wouldn't change a moment of the life I've shared with your *dat*. I'm grateful for him, and for you and your *bruder* and Joshua. To think I might have missed out on all of that, because I thought love was supposed to be butterflies and puppy dog stares."

Butterflies and puppy dog stares.

Those five words followed Zeb as he walked back out to the barn to tend to the horses. Is that what he'd had with Suzanne? Maybe it had started that way, but it had turned into a real love, a mature love.

And then that love had been yanked away.

His *mamm* might be right about second love, but personally, he didn't think it was something that he would ever find out about in his own life.

He'd found childcare for Josh. He'd found a part-time job. One way or another, he would get a loan on this farm so that he could raise his son as he'd been raised, in the same place he'd been raised. But second love? Nope. He didn't think so. He was pretty sure he was meant to be alone forever.

Chapter Four

The five Yoder women were seated in Eunice's bedroom, supposedly helping her unpack. She'd unpacked the night she'd told her father about Zeb's proposal. Still, her *schweschdern* had insisted on coming over the following Tuesday. Sarah, Becca, Eunice, Bethany and Ada were all squeezed into the twelve-by-twelve room. Plus, Lydia, Bethany's *doschder*, and Mary, Becca's *doschder*, were offering a steady stream of real and made-up words. Both girls would turn four years old in December. At the moment, they were using all the colors in the crayon box to create rainbow pictures.

Coloring pictures. How could they be coloring pictures already? Wasn't it just the other day that they'd all waited at the hospital for them to be born? How could they possibly be almost four years old? Time was such a strange thing. Eunice often felt that some days lasted forever. Some nights were even longer. But the years? The years flew by.

They all seemed to be aware of how quickly things were changing, and so they'd decided to have a family meeting that morning. In truth, they just wanted to spend some time together.

Eunice loved getting caught up with her *schweschdern*. Though they lived fairly close to one another and saw each other at least once a week, it still felt like they didn't have time together. Time to just sit and talk. Time to be together.

"How are you feeling, Sarah?" Becca was peering at their oldest *schweschder* closely, as if to detect any problem she might be experiencing.

"Being pregnant is *wunderbaar*," Sarah admitted. "So far, at least. I pray it stays that way, but I remember how it was for you all, and I'm—"

"Older," they all chimed in.

Everyone had been surprised and thrilled to learn that Sarah was pregnant. More than once she'd shared her worry that she wouldn't be a *mamm*. She'd feared that particular dream wouldn't come true for her, since she had recently turned thirty-two. And then—suddenly—she was. Noah had been so excited at the news that he'd nearly driven the buggy off the road when she'd told him.

Eunice loved that story.

She loved all of her family's stories.

"Whatcha looking at, sis?" Ada poked Eunice's foot with her own. She had an eight-month-old boy who was with his *dat* at the moment. Both Peter and Ethan were the cinnamon of Ada's life. Ada was on a cinnamon kick, so it was the highest compliment she could give.

"This room," Eunice admitted. "I can't believe I've lived in this same room all of my life."

"Sort of," Becca said. She smiled at her little girl, Mary, who showed her the rainbow she'd drawn. Becca's son, Abram, was seven months old. He tried to reach for the picture, but Mary plopped back down on the floor with the drawing and managed to keep it out of his grasp.

"He slobbers," she whispered to Lydia.

Ada was apparently still thinking about what Eunice had

said. "Remember when we all moved into the same room? When Aaron and Ethan's house had that fire?"

Bethany started laughing, and baby Daniel reached up to pat his mother's face. "The only way to get out of the room was to step over—"

"Or on," Becca chimed in.

"Or on someone else." Bethany rocked her son, a smile wreathing her face. "I rather miss those days."

"I think we all do," Sarah said. "Look at us now. Five girls. Four husbands. Five children—"

"And one on the way," Eunice pointed out.

"And one on the way." Sarah began to blink rapidly.

"Uh-oh. She's spilling her feelings." Ada jumped up and fetched her a tissue. "Which is way better than having a heart of rock."

"Stone," her *schweschder* mouthed, but no one corrected her. They were beyond correcting Ada's misquotes. Sarah had even begun listing them in a journal.

"Back to you, Eunice." Bethany cocked her head and gave her full attention to Eunice. "That was a very close call you experienced. I'd bought extra stamps so I could write you every day."

"I was actually all packed and ready to go," Eunice admitted. "How is it that my entire life fit into two small boxes and a suitcase?"

"It's not as if we have a closet full of clothes." Ada plopped on the bed. "When it's time to hit the buggy lane—"

"Hit the road," Becca whispered.

Ada wagged her index finger. "When it's time to hit the buggy lane, Amish folk can pack fast. But how do you feel about everything, Eunice?"

"I'm relieved, I guess."

"About staying, sure. But how do you feel about minding Zeb's son?"

"Fine, I guess."

"And you're not…interested in him in a romantic way?" Bethany wiggled her eyebrows.

Which started all four of Eunice's *schweschdern* talking about Zeb and laughing and insinuating that this entire situation was something that it wasn't.

Eunice had to whistle to get their attention. "It's not like that. Zeb was desperate to find someone to keep Josh. He heard that I needed a job, so he thought we could help each other out."

"We'll stop teasing, Eunice." Sarah stood and arched her back. "But we're excited about all the changes in your life. Our lives are centered around home—cooking and cleaning and babies. We don't get out as much as you do. That's why we have to live through you, little sister."

Live through her?

Eunice's life was the most tame of all of them.

Some days she had trouble keeping up with all of the changes in her family. Since Sarah had learned she was pregnant, Noah and his parents had made the decision to add on to their home. Ada's and Bethany's husbands were brothers, and the house on Huckleberry Lane had gone through quite a renovation in the last few years. Ada and her husband, Ethan, had made the decision to build a separate house, allowing Bethany and Aaron to remain in the original home with their two children. Becca and Gideon lived on the same property as Eunice and her *dat*, but even they were talking about building another barn.

It seemed as if only Eunice's life had stayed the same.

Wake in the morning.

Walk out to the barn and work on her latest project.

Rinse and repeat.

They suddenly heard the sound of horse hooves, and they all went to the window—standing in birth order as they always did. Eunice automatically went to the middle of the group. She'd always been comfortable in the middle—two older *schweschdern* and two younger. It had seemed the perfect place to be. Now she wondered about that.

Perhaps if she'd been first or last she would have done something with her life. The middle was comfortable. She'd allowed herself to become quite content watching her older and younger siblings go about their lives. She'd become an observer and somewhere in the last five or even ten years she'd stopped participating. At least it felt that way now.

"Looks like he's here, sis. Zeb, the handsome friend but not boyfriend, and his adorable son." Bethany tossed her a knowing smile. "Why's he coming by today? I thought you didn't start watching Josh until next week."

"Trial run," Eunice explained. "He thought we should spend an hour together just to make sure everything will work out."

"Ah." Becca pulled Eunice into a hug and then they were all in one big jumble with their arms around one another, laughing and crying and assuring Mary and Lydia that nothing was wrong.

But it was as they were headed down the stairs that Sarah pulled Eunice aside. "You're going to be fine."

"I know."

"Stop worrying."

There was no point in denying it. Sarah had always been able to read her like a book. "Okay."

It was when Sarah put her arms around her and pulled her close that the tears began to sting Eunice's eyes. By the time she pulled away, they were coursing down her cheeks. Eunice could hear Zeb knocking on the front door, her nieces laughing and running, her *schweschdern* greeting Zeb. She could hear it all, but it was as if those things were happening very far away.

Sarah nudged her shoulder. "Worst fears."

It was a game they'd begun playing long ago.

"Something terrible will happen to Josh, and I won't know what to do."

"That's not even remotely possible. You can see Becca's front door from here. She's happy to help you. What else?"

Eunice only shook her head.

How could she put her biggest fears into words? It wasn't just the two new jobs. She thought she could learn to use a cash register. She thought one child couldn't be that hard to care for.

But all of the rush and worry of the last thirty days had finally worn her down. It had worked its way into her mind and her subconscious. She'd actually dreamed the night before that she was alone on a boat in a vast sea, and she couldn't figure out which way to paddle.

She didn't need Ezekiel or a counselor to tell her what that dream meant.

She was the only one left. She was the only remaining burden on her father. She would live here in her childhood home until he was gone. Then she'd be pushed off into a *grossmammi haus*—in her case perhaps it might be called an *aenti*'s *haus*—and one of her siblings' growing families would move into the main house. She could see it all play out like some nightmare flashing before her eyes on a never-ending loop.

But that wasn't going to happen today. Today she would learn to be an excellent caregiver for one five-year-old boy.

And Monday morning, she would learn to work in a yarn shop. She could do these things.

So she squared her shoulders, plastered on a smile and allowed Sarah to wipe away her tears. "I'm only emotional because when we're all together, I remember how much I miss everyone."

"You do realize we're all right here in Shipshe, right?" Sarah tucked her arm through Eunice's.

"*Ya.* And you'll stop by to make sure I haven't put Joshua on a roof or forgotten to feed him."

"I definitely will. I'll make a real pest of myself."

"*Gut.*"

"Exactly." By the time they arrived on the porch where everyone else was waiting, Eunice had her emotions in check. She squatted down and said hello to Joshua.

"I'm staying with you, just while *Dat*'s on tour."

"Exactly."

"Do you have any kids?"

"I don't, but…"

At that moment both Mary and Lydia burst through the kaleidoscope of their mother's skirts and launched into a game of tag.

Joshua looked surprised.

He looked as if he'd thought he was the only child in the world.

"You can play with them if you want."

Josh glanced over at his *dat*, who nodded once.

Stepping closer to Eunice, Zeb lowered his voice and said, "Just don't let him out of your sight for more than a minute."

"Got it, boss."

Zeb said his goodbyes to her *schweschdern*, then hurried away. Either he was late, or he didn't know what to do with a porch full of Yoder women.

Eunice stood in the middle of Ada and Becca and Bethany and Sarah as Zeb drove down their lane. She could do this. She could babysit a kid. Good grief, girls ten years younger than her did as much.

Ada hooked an arm through hers, and they all followed the children around to the backyard. "Tell us about your life, Eunice."

"Nothing to tell."

"What are you working on?" Becca asked.

"Nothing, at the moment." It sounded pitiful even to her own ears. "I guess when people heard I was moving they stopped bringing their broken items, and now with two jobs—"

"You won't have much time for tinkering," Bethany said. "You're going to be one busy woman, sis."

Eunice felt the need, in that moment of sunshine and laughter and family, to tell the truth. "I'd rather be in the barn. I know what I'm doing in there. I'm comfortable in there. Why does everything have to change?"

"Change can be *gut*," Ada said. "Think of how busy you'll be."

"I don't want to be more busy."

"And we don't want you to be stuck in that barn. Now *kapp* up and carry on."

"Chin up," Becca murmured, tossing their youngest *schweschder* a smile.

"You never know what's going to happen in the next year or month or week." Becca's voice took on a melancholy tone. "Five years ago none of us were married. We certainly didn't have any children."

Ada laughed. "The biggest thing I had on my mind when I left home was learning to cook."

"Did you?" Eunice asked.

"Did I what?"

"Learn to cook?"

"Yup. Beth insisted that I make dinner every other day."

"Just because we live together doesn't mean I'm going to cook for everyone, plus you needed to learn." Bethany tossed a knowing look at her youngest *schweschder*. "After a dozen burnt suppers, your ability to concentrate improved."

"I was like a puppy that had learned a new trick," Ada admitted.

"Old dog?" Eunice asked.

"Have you tried teaching Gizmo a new trick?"

They all turned to stare at the old mixed breed who was lying in a patch of sunlight. The dog rolled onto his back, all four feet up in the air, and whimpered. Which caused everyone to laugh, even the babies.

It was a bittersweet moment for Eunice.

Life was changing so fast, and there was so much love and joy in this group that she couldn't help pausing and appreciating all that they had. Most importantly, they had each other.

On the other hand, a voice in the back of her mind whispered, *This will change too. Everything changes*.

It was with that thought echoing through her mind that she said goodbye to her siblings who were scattering in their different directions.

Which left her alone with young Joshua.

Zeb had said he'd only be gone an hour. He'd even called this first short stay a *trial run*. What was she going to do with a child she barely knew for an hour? Could she really do this? Watch over a child? And what would happen if she failed? Would her *dat* buy her yet another bus ticket to Kentucky? She wanted to crawl into bed and pull the quilt over her head. She wanted to walk into the barn and lose herself in a project.

She couldn't do either of those things because Josh was looking up at her expectantly.

"Want to play catch?" she asked.

He grinned and slipped his small hand into hers. Something in Eunice melted. Some frozen chunk that she hadn't even realized she was carrying around turned into a puddle.

"Sure, Eunice. But I have to warn you, I can throw a ball pretty hard."

"Consider me duly warned."

Something about Josh's carefree demeanor eased her worries the slightest bit. She might still end up moving to Kentucky. Who knew? But she wasn't moving there today. Today she was going to play catch with her friend's son. Maybe she should focus on that, and let tomorrow take care of itself.

She could certainly try.

Zeb's first tour was on Wednesday, October 16. His parents had left town the day before. He still couldn't believe it. How had everything happened so fast? He and Samuel and Josh had driven them to the bus station and watched them wave goodbye. Still, he couldn't believe it. That afternoon, the moving company showed up to collect their things. He was caught in the middle of a whirlwind, and he had no idea how to escape it. He tried to get up the next morning and pretend everything was normal. He attempted to cook oatmeal for Joshua, burned it and served the boy cold cereal instead.

The morning had flown by, and then it was time to take Josh to Eunice's. He'd had a week after their trial run to get used to the idea of leaving Joshua with Eunice, but still his stomach was in knots as he drove away from the Yoder home. He'd sought her out the Sunday before, which was an off-Sunday, to give her a list.

He had thought—still believed—that it was a very practical list of how to care for a five-year-old boy.

Eunice had taken one look at the list, folded the sheet of paper, put it in her apron pocket and walked away. What did that mean? Had he offended her? Had he not given enough instructions? Why were women so hard to understand?

Soon he was at the Amish market, and a half hour later he was shepherding a dozen *Englisch* tourists through the Behind the Scenes Market Tour. For a few moments of that hour and a half, he actually forgot to worry about Josh. He was surprised to find he enjoyed the *Englischers* and their questions.

Do Amish have cell phones? Some do.

Do local Amish families have indoor plumbing? Absolutely.

Did he wish he had a television or a computer in his home? Not even a little.

He took them behind the scenes so they were able to see how the animals were cared for at the Backyard Barnyard which was located on the Market's property and offered a small petting zoo for guests. They watched how auction items were tagged, toured the pretty little RV park and stopped by the kitchen area where food was prepared for the canteen.

Zeb imagined much of it was like what they'd see at any business establishment. But they oohed over the girl cleaning windows with a crumbled-up piece of newspaper. "Less streaking than paper towels," Claire King had explained.

They were surprised that there was no microwave in the kitchen. Thrilled to find that the eggs laid by the chickens in the Backyard Barnyard were used in the canteen's kitchen. Very happy with the free single-serving pies they received from the Fry Pie booth.

The tourists exclaimed they were very happy with the

tour, tipped generously and overall were an easy group to guide. Zeb wondered if every day would go that well. It wasn't until he was in the buggy again, headed back out to the Yoder farm, that he thought to worry about Josh.

He practically let the mare break into a trot once he turned into the Yoders' lane. When he called out "Whoa," Beauty tossed her head and neighed in response, then eyed him as if they'd been playing a game.

This was no game.

Where was his son?

He'd thought they'd be waiting on the porch for him to arrive, but Eunice and Josh weren't on the porch. They weren't in the backyard near the garden and the swings. He walked around the house, then eyed the barn. Surely they weren't in there. It was a fine October day. Why wouldn't she be outside with the boy?

When he pushed open the door to the barn, afternoon sunlight spilled across the floor. Eunice was standing at the workbench, pieces of wood spread out in front of her. Josh was holding a can of linseed oil in one hand and a cookie in the other.

"Dat." He looked up in surprise. "I'm helping, Eunice."

"I see that."

"And I'm eating a snack."

"I see that too."

"What happened to your tour?"

"Nothing happened. Everything went fine."

"You're done already?" Josh popped the last piece of cookie in his mouth. "Seems like I just got here."

"It does seem that way," Eunice agreed, reaching over to mess Josh's hair and getting a bit of grease on his forehead in the process. "You've been a good helper."

"Thanks!" He hopped off the stool he'd been perched atop and grinned at Zeb. "I'm a *gut* helper."

"So I heard. Say, Josh. Could you give me a minute to talk to Eunice?"

"*Ya.* I'll go and say goodbye to Gizmo."

"Probably lying on, around or under the front porch," Eunice called after him.

"Got it."

Zeb tried not to wince at the thought of his son crawling under the porch. There was no telling what was under there.

"Good tour?" Eunice asked, wiping her hands on a greasy rag that couldn't possibly make her hands any cleaner.

"It was. But listen, Eunice. I thought we talked about this."

"Talked about what?"

He tamped down what he wanted to say which was *Weren't you listening at all?* Instead, he stared at the floor for a five count, then plastered on a smile and looked up. "Did you even read the list I gave you?"

She walked over to the cork board, pulled out a push pin and retrieved the list, setting it on the workbench in front of him. "This, you mean?"

"Yes, that. Number 3 plainly says that Joshua should not be working around your tools. He could get hurt."

"With linseed oil and a piece of sandpaper?"

He snatched the list from her and stormed out the door of the barn.

Eunice followed closely on his heels. "Seriously. Are you going to tell me that you think he could be hurt dripping linseed oil onto a rag, while I work it into the pieces of that cradle?"

Zeb took in a deep breath. Blew it out. "Didn't realize it was a cradle."

"For Sarah. *Ya.* It is."

"It's just that I don't want him around your tools. There are sharp things, solar-powered things, any number of ways he could be hurt."

Eunice sank onto the bench and studied him as he paced back and forth in front of the barn. Finally, she said, "Wow. You are wound tight."

"He's my son, Eunice. My only…" Zeb blinked away the tears. They embarrassed him. His love and fears for Josh were like a heavy coat that he wore every single day, every single hour, every single minute. And running beneath all of that he sincerely wished that he wasn't having this conversation, wished that he didn't look as vulnerable as he felt.

"Hey." She waited until he looked up. "I get that."

"Do you?"

"Yes. He's your son. You lost your wife. You don't want anything to happen to Josh, but Zeb…" Now she stood, walked right up to him, took the piece of paper from his hand and waved it in front of his face so that he had to step back. "This list is ridiculous."

"No, it isn't."

"Yes, it is. What about number 2? Feed him? Do you really think I don't know to feed a child who is hungry?"

"You could forget."

"And number 1 is to not let him near wild animals. What wild animals do you think Josh could find on a farm in northern Indiana?"

Zeb snatched the piece of paper out of her hand, not wanting her to berate him about each item. They'd made perfectly good sense when he'd written them down. They only sounded silly because Eunice read them in a sarcastic way.

She reached out and touched his arm, and he jerked away as if she'd touched him with a branding iron.

"Sorry." She stared out across the fields, rubbed the muscles on the back of her neck, then turned and walked toward the end of the barn.

Zeb really had no choice but to follow.

"Look at him, Zeb. He's a normal boy, playing with an old dog. Now I understand that number 7 says to keep him away from stray cats and dogs, but this is Gizmo we're talking about. Gizmo is as sweet and gentle as they come. He's also old. His running days are over. It isn't like he could chase Josh down and gnaw on his ankle."

Zeb didn't want to laugh at that, but it was a funny image.

"We had a *gut* day today."

Eunice turned to look at him, and in a flash, Zeb realized how pretty she was, how innocent. Eunice Yoder had no idea how quickly tragedy could strike.

"Josh and I got along fine. You need to trust both of us."

"Trust doesn't come that easily for me."

"*Ya*, well, maybe that's something you could work on."

Instead of answering, he nodded curtly, and muttered, "See you tomorrow."

His mood didn't improve when he had to hear Josh chatter on about Eunice all the way home. How Eunice makes the best cookies. How Eunice showed him how to make homemade lemonade. How Eunice knows a lot about building stuff. Isn't Eunice the best?

Zeb didn't know what he'd expected.

For Josh to be sitting in the shade of the barn, crying and waiting for his father all day? For him to say he'd rather stay with his *grossmammi*? But Josh didn't do or say any of those things. He was a five-year-old boy who had played with an old dog, eaten cookies and lemonade, and helped out in the barn. And he couldn't wait to go back the next day.

That night, dinner was burned bologna sandwiches.

And though Zeb was exhausted, it took him hours to fall

asleep. He kept thinking of Suzanne. He kept wondering why his life had turned out this way. Kept worrying over how he was supposed to raise a boy without a mother. Or even a grandmother, for that matter.

The one thing he knew was that he'd have to push through the next day, and the day after that, and the day after that. Such was life, he supposed. He'd find a way to do it and even plaster on a smile—for Joshua.

But he wouldn't enjoy it. Of that, he was certain.

Chapter Five

Like his church in Lancaster, the Indiana community here in Shipshe met twice a month. There were church Sundays and there were off-Sundays. Zeb wasn't sure which weekend he dreaded most.

Sundays when they held church services had begun to feel like a job interview. Various women approached him, asking him a myriad of questions. Was he adjusting to life in Shipshe? How was Josh doing since his grandparents had moved? Was he planning to stay in the area? Their interest was obvious, and he felt as if he should warn them away but never could quite find the words. Worse, sometimes their parents approached as if they were trying to decide whether he was a worthy suitor.

He wasn't worthy, and he wasn't a suitor.

He had no intention of dating, let alone marrying.

Not now. Maybe not ever.

Weekends when they had an off-Sunday should have been better, but somehow the smaller groups only increased the pressure he felt.

This Sunday, they had been invited to the Yoder home. With Amos's five daughters, four sons-in-law and five *grandkinner*, it was a big group. Add to that mix Zeb, Samuel, Josh, plus two other families that had been invited, and it felt like a crowd.

It didn't escape his notice that both of the other families—the Gingerichs and the Lapps—had unmarried daughters. The third time he was cornered to answer questions about his job, his prospects and his son, he snagged Josh's hand and said, "Let's go to the barn."

Actually they went behind the barn, where the horses had been set loose. Josh clamored to the top of the wooden fence and perched on the top rung. Zeb stayed close to make sure the boy didn't fall.

He wasn't exactly surprised when Eunice stepped out of the barn.

"You're hiding too?" he asked.

She raised her eyebrows in mock surprise. "Who would I be hiding from?"

Zeb jerked his head back toward the group.

Eunice's smile was affirmation enough. "I wouldn't call it hiding—not exactly."

"I want to hide." Josh scrambled down from the fence. "Bet you can't find me."

"Bet we can," Eunice said. "And don't think I'll go easy on you because you're short."

"I'm not short."

"Okay, I won't go easy on you because you're young."

"I'm five, Eunice." He held up his hand, fingers splayed. "That isn't young. And I can count to twenty. Don't look until I say *twenty*. I'll say it real loud."

Then he dashed into the barn, shouting, "One, two, three…"

"Anything in there he can hurt himself on?"

"Probably."

Zeb had been staring out at the horses. Now he jerked his head toward Eunice only to see her smiling.

"I'm kidding. He's been coming here for two weeks. He knows what tools are off-limits. You sure are jumpy."

"*Ya.* Five-year-old boys can do that to you."

They both glanced toward the barn as Josh continued to shout numbers. "Twelve, thirteen…"

"He counts well."

"That he does." Zeb turned away from the field and the horses which only made him wish he could be out there instead of stuck in a crowd of people. Crossing his arms, he leaned against the fence, studying Eunice.

She waited.

Eunice was like that. She didn't push a guy to talk if he didn't want to. It was one of the many reasons they'd been friends for so long.

"What are *you* hiding from?" he finally asked.

"Are you kidding? Both the Gingerich family and the Lapps have unmarried sons."

Zeb couldn't help laughing. It started small like a grunt and grew until he was clutching his side.

"What's so funny?"

He pointed a finger at her while he tried to catch his breath.

"Are you laughing at me?"

He could tell she was trying to sound offended. In truth, Eunice didn't offend easily. She was very even-tempered unless you misplaced one of her tools or didn't return one you'd borrowed. He'd only made that mistake once.

"What's so funny?"

"Both families also have unmarried daughters."

Understanding dawned on her face. "You think my *dat* is setting you up?"

"Do you think he's setting *you* up?"

"I wouldn't put either one past him." Eunice worked some dirt from under her nail. "After marrying off four of his daughters, he thinks he's an expert at matchmaking. The fact that he'd had no success was one of the reasons he nearly sent me to Kentucky. Now that I'm staying, seems he's back to his old tricks."

Zeb managed to wrangle his laughter under control. It felt good to laugh though. It had been a long time. Why was that? Why was he determined to be so dour? Even he felt it—the unnaturalness of his moods, but it had become a habit now, and habits were difficult to change. He shook off that thought, cocked his head and asked, "So? Is that so bad? I mean all of your *schweschdern* seem happy. Maybe Amos is good at matchmaking."

"No, thank you."

"No, thank you because…"

"And now you sound like *Dat.*"

He was about to answer when he heard Josh holler from the barn, "Did you hear me say *twenty*? Are you looking yet?"

Zeb pushed away from the fence. "I guess we should go look for him."

"Or we could leave him there, grab some desserts and hide on the back porch."

He wasn't usually a laugh-behind-the-barn, touchy-feely kind of person, but this was Eunice. She'd watched Josh seven times now, and nothing terrible had happened. Zeb was starting to think this arrangement just might work out.

So he snagged her arm and pulled her with him into the barn. "See, that's something a person who doesn't have a child would say. Once you have a child, you're blessed with an enormous sense of guilt that won't allow you to do such things."

"Sounds terrible."

"Some days it is."

It was pretty easy to find Josh, and true to her word, Eunice didn't cut him any breaks. She walked over to the work-bench, bent down and said, "Want to try again?"

"Yes. This time I'll hide outside. One, two, three…" And he was gone, running back out into the sunlight.

"Lots of energy," Eunice noted.

"You have no idea."

"How are you doing?" Eunice asked. She waited, study-ing him, and then added, "I mean how are you *really* doing?"

From anyone else, that question would have produced an odd resentment that he'd been nurturing for just about two years now. Coming from Eunice though, he couldn't work up any indignation. "Terrible."

"Ya?"

"Every day is…hard."

She didn't respond right away to that. Didn't say it would get better. Didn't lecture him that it was time to move on. Instead she swiped at a clean workspace with a rag. "I don't understand why life has to be so hard. Why did my *mamm* die? Why did your *fraa* die? Why is life like this?"

"Hey. It's not all bad." Zeb realized the irony of him say-ing that. He was trying to cheer up Eunice versus the other way around. That was backward. Wasn't it? What did she have to feel blue about? Sure, she'd lost her *mamm*, but that had been so many years ago.

"What? What did you just think of?"

He gulped but knew there was no use in denying it. "That you're my age, and you're still grieving the loss of your *mamm*."

"So?"

"So, will Josh carry around that burden all of his life? Will he still be missing his *mamm* when he's twenty-five?"

"Maybe it'll be different, because he's a guy."

"Meaning?"

"You all tend to ignore your feelings, right? I mean… I think I read that in some *Englisch* magazine. Ten ways to find out what your man is really feeling."

"You read *Englisch* magazines?"

"What else are you supposed to do while you're waiting in the checkout line?"

"Fair enough."

She nodded toward the area outside the barn. "Your son yelled *twenty* like five minutes ago."

"Right." Zeb squared his shoulders and walked outside.

Eunice reached for his arm. "Don't worry about Josh. I mean, I know you are going to worry about him, but don't worry about that. What you just said—I don't think he'll be grieving until he's twenty-five."

"But you still miss your *mamm*."

"Of course I do, same as you'd always miss an arm if you lost it, but that's not…" She glanced away, a rosiness creeping into her cheeks. "I'm just in a funk. It's not all about *Mamm*. It's more about the mess I've made of my life."

"You have?"

Josh's voice interrupted whatever Eunice might have said when he shouted, "Are you guys even looking?"

"He's over behind the water trough," Eunice said. "You want to find him this time, or should I?"

"How about we do it together?"

"Deal."

"And then we'll get dessert."

"Dessert does make most situations seem better."

"Never makes things worse."

But as they ambled over to the trough, where he could see his son's straw hat peeking out from the corner, Zeb couldn't help wondering why Eunice thought she'd made a mess of her life. As far as he could see, she'd made some pretty good

choices. Never falling in love might have its advantages—
at least he assumed she'd never fallen in love. She'd never
mentioned anyone that she cared about.

He admired that.

If you never put your heart out there, then it couldn't get
broken.

And at that moment, Eunice's decision to be alone
sounded like a very wise choice indeed. Perhaps he could
borrow a page from her book. Maybe he could guard his
heart against ever caring for anyone again—in a romantic
way. Of course he cared for Josh and his parents and even
his older brother who frustrated him to the point of distrac-
tion most days. But romance? Uh-uh. He didn't think he'd
ever do that again. Even Amos couldn't set up a match that
would break his resolve.

As they walked back to the dessert table, then found a
place to sit on a blanket under the maple tree, Zeb couldn't
help noticing something else. Josh was very comfortable
around Eunice. He sat close to her. Offered her one of his
brownies. Pulled a folded-up piece of paper from his pocket
and showed her his most recent drawing. This time it was
an old barn, with a stick girl beside it wielding a hammer
in one hand and what might have been a bottle of linseed
oil in the other.

His son was growing attached to Eunice Yoder. Maybe it
was due to the lack of any other motherly figure in his life.
Zeb could only hope that Eunice wasn't planning on going
anywhere because he did not want to see his son experience
another loss.

As for Amos's matchmaking attempts—if that was what
today was—he should save his efforts for someone interested. There was an assumption in Amish communities that
widows and widowers would remarry. They'd wait an appro-

priate amount of time. Find a partner who fit the description. Build a life together.

But Zeb had been there and done that. He had absolutely no intention of doing it again.

Eunice was surprised to find that she was enjoying watching Josh three afternoons a week. The kid was easy to be around. He reminded her of Zeb when they'd been young. Zeb had possessed the same energy and impish grin. Caring for Josh felt much more natural than she thought it would. What had she been so worried about?

Her other job—at the yarn shop job—was proving a little more difficult. Mrs. Lancaster had opened The Stitch & Skein two years earlier, and she was very particular about how things should be done. Eunice didn't blame her. She, herself, was meticulous about where her tools went in the barn.

The problem was that she knew nothing about knitting or crocheting. She'd thought the word *stitch* always referred to quilting. And the word *skein*? She'd never heard of it.

"A skein is yarn in an oblong shape, dear."

"What other shape would yarn possibly be in?"

"A ball or a hank, of course. If you went to a craft store in a large city, you'd find a good many of the yarns are wound in balls, which can make knitting with them a bit difficult, unless they're a center pull."

The conversation went on like that until Eunice lost interest, which honestly didn't take very long. Just when she thought she'd caught on to the lingo, she realized there was a lot more to yarn work than talking about it. There was texture and thickness and color. There was any number of ways for her to make mistakes when trying to help shoppers.

When a customer walked into the store and asked where their hanks of yarn were, Eunice could point them in the right direction. But when they wanted opinions on what colors went with what other colors, she might as well have been color blind.

She'd recently convinced a woman that pink, red and orange would make a lovely sweater. Mrs. Lancaster intervened before the woman actually purchased the yarn, which was a good thing because Eunice was not clear on the return policy. In this case, her boss walked off muttering, "Those colors together could have given that poor woman a migraine."

Eunice had never suffered a migraine, but she thought she might start if she had to hear yet another conversation about the benefits of alpaca over angora. Ugh. Who would even notice?

She longed to be in her barn, staring into the heart of a windmill.

But she'd made a deal, and she planned to stick with it. The alternative was Kentucky, and she was not ready to take that step. Still—yarn shop? She would have been a better fit for almost any other job. Actually, she would have been better fit for a man's job. Sometimes the gender stereotypes in their community scraped against her heart. Was it her fault that she enjoyed engines and grease more than baking and sewing?

"I can't remember what the point of my having this job is," she'd complained to Zeb the next Wednesday when he'd come to pick up Joshua. "I'm not making enough money to support myself, and it's not as if I'm going to meet a man in a yarn shop."

"Ah." Zeb looked uncomfortable. It was the same expression he always wore anytime she brought up dating or women or marriage.

"That's it? That's all you've got? Ah?"

"It's just that you're not at the yarn shop to catch a man. You're there to prove you can take care of yourself. Right?

That you can earn a steady income. I thought that was your *dat*'s alternative to marrying you off."

"Don't say that."

"What?"

"Marrying off. Makes me sound like a..." She decided to abandon that train of thought. "Okay. You're right. I'm proving myself financially independent. Something no Amish woman has ever been."

Zeb did that thing where he tried to hide a smile.

"What?"

"Nothing."

"Say it."

"Mrs. Lancaster, the woman you work for, is a financially independent Amish woman."

"True. Guess I hadn't thought of her that way." Eunice attempted to rub a spot of engine oil off her left hand. She'd worked on a lawn mower. How did she manage to get so dirty working on small engines? That would be one advantage of being a knitter, you rarely had to deal with grease under your fingernails.

"We're both in a funk," Zeb admitted.

"Ain't that the truth."

"Maybe we should do something about it."

"Like what?"

"I don't know. Something besides work and..."

"Work." Eunice was nodding now. "Say. The antique tractor show is this weekend. My shift at the yarn place ends at three on Saturday. Want to meet me over there?"

"I guess it might be something Josh would like."

"Are you kidding? Josh loves engines."

Zeb pinned her with a glare.

She raised her hands in mock surrender. "Not that I've let him near one. I'm just saying. The boy is naturally curious."

"Don't forget the safety list."

She rolled her eyes, then closed them, attempting to count to ten and making it halfway. "Great. We'll meet at the entrance to the antique tractor show a bit after three."

"Sounds *gut*."

They were talking as they walked out of the barn. Josh was giving his customary goodbye hug to Gizmo. As they continued to talk about the tractor show, Josh launched himself at Eunice's legs, wrapping her in a hug. He was an affectionate kid and did this at least twice a visit. Each time, something in Eunice's heart thrummed. She'd never thought she wanted to marry and have children. She'd never really considered it because she'd always felt like the proverbial square peg that was supposed to fit in a round hole. But when Josh hugged her and smiled up at her, she wondered if perhaps she should have tried harder to have a conventional life. And then the bigger question always followed those thoughts—was it too late?

Eunice straightened the straw hat on his head, then said, "See you tomorrow, kid."

"Yup. See you."

Josh ran to the buggy, stopping to offer Beauty a piece of carrot that he pulled from his pocket.

"Now where did he get that?"

"Helped me in the garden earlier."

"Ah."

Eunice stopped halfway between the barn and Zeb's buggy. "I just remembered what I meant to ask you. *Dat* needs me to help out at the market tomorrow—fall festival crowds and all that. I think I'll be in the barnyard. Think I could watch Josh there?"

Zeb looked as if he didn't like that idea at all, but he was apparently unable to come up with any valid reason to say no. "I guess. It's just that—"

"We need to be careful. *Ya*. I know. I read the list every night," she teased. "No sharp tools. Remember to feed him. Yada yada yada."

Zeb attempted a laugh, but it fell pretty flat.

"Listen. If it bothers you, I'll tell *Dat* I can't do it. We can meet here as usual."

"*Nein*. I'm being overprotective."

Eunice could feel her eyebrows pop up.

"What?"

"I just thought…well, I thought you weren't aware."

"That I'm overprotective? Trust me. I'm aware."

Which she thought might be a good thing. She stood there waving as he and Josh climbed into the buggy, then drove back down the lane. If she were truthful with herself—and what was the point in being anything but—she did enjoy the variety of her life now.

As for the little boy hanging one arm out of the buggy and waving at her, he was quickly claiming a large portion of her heart. She needed to be careful about that though. Zeb would marry again one day, and when he did, she would be replaced. No one needed a babysitter for a child when they had a wife.

Somehow that thought stole all the sunshine from her day.

Chapter Six

Eunice spent the early hours of the next morning attending to things around the house so that she could spend the afternoon at the market. The fall festival was always a huge success, and she found herself whistling as she hurried through her chores, then changed clothes. She'd never worked at the Amish market on a permanent basis, but she'd helped out occasionally—most often at the Christmas market.

This year's autumn celebration promised to be the biggest yet. Her *dat* had put out a call for all hands on deck. Though none of them had ever been sailing, Eunice, her *schweschdern* and her *bruders*-in-law all understood what he meant.

After at least a decade of drawing large, steady crowds, the market was growing even bigger. Perhaps because her *dat* was implementing new ideas. With each new son-in-law, he'd expanded the market.

Gideon had taken on the role of assistant manager, and later married Becca. Aaron was in charge of the RV park. He'd first worked there with her *schweschder* Bethany, who was now a stay-at-home mom. Ethan covered special auctions that had been added randomly throughout the year. They always drew large crowds as well as articles in the paper. Ethan was married to Ada, something Eunice hadn't seen coming. And Noah was in charge of a work crew that oversaw additions and renovations. Noah and Sarah had been married the year before.

Four new sons-in-law.

Four market expansions.

And now Zeb was in charge of *Englisch* tours at the market. Yeah. She definitely could read the writing on the wall, and though she'd warned her *dat* that it wouldn't work, she couldn't help being glad that Zeb had taken the job. Maybe it would improve his outlook. Maybe he'd find something to look forward to, other than his son. It was plain that Zeb adored Joshua, but she suspected Zeb was missing adult conversation. Apparently his *bruder* wasn't around much, which meant it was just Zeb and Joshua at home alone most of the time.

Was he also missing the companionship he'd had with his wife? Eunice hadn't really known Suzanne, though they'd met at the wedding. She found herself wondering how he had adjusted to being a widower. How did one go from being part of a couple to being alone?

Zeb might not think he wanted to date another woman.

He was probably hiding on his farm much like she had been hiding in the barn. At least the tour groups had forced him out into the world for three afternoons a week.

Maybe he'd meet a potential spouse on one of the tours.

Eunice had heard of *Englischers* converting to the Amish faith, though it was rare.

Despite his hesitant attitude toward dating again, Eunice thought that would change in time. She suspected that he would want to marry again, once his heart had healed. He was good-looking, smart and kind. He would have no problem finding a woman to court. He'd have no problem falling in love. He'd find another woman like Suzanne—someone who was traditional. Someone who would be satisfied being a homemaker and having a large family. Someone who would provide Josh with plenty of brothers and sisters.

Zeb fit in as far as the community was concerned. Eunice didn't. And while she had thought she was used to that, some days it rankled her more than others.

As she harnessed Oreo to the buggy and set out to the market, Eunice couldn't help appreciating the beautiful autumn day. The leaves on the trees had yet to fall, but they offered a dazzling array of orange, red and yellow color. She passed yards sporting scarecrows and jolly pumpkins. As she drew closer to town, she noticed that every shop window was decked out with harvest displays.

She wished that her mood could match what she was seeing. She knew how to put on a good show for people, smiled when she was supposed to, asked about their jobs and families. Her mood didn't always match her face though. In truth, she felt a restless kind of dissatisfaction that was like an itch in the middle of her back—impossible to reach. It was exhausting.

Maybe something was wrong with her. Maybe she was sick. She didn't feel sick though. She simply felt…adrift. That was the word. As if she had no idea if she was going this way or that.

Fortunately, Oreo had no such reservations.

Without any direction from Eunice, the mare turned into the parking area for the market.

The Shipshewana Outdoor Market was usually only open on Tuesdays and Wednesdays from May through September. Auctions—both livestock and antiques—continued throughout the year, but there wasn't the normal display of vendors once the summer season had closed.

For the annual fall festival, they opened the entire market from Thursday through Saturday, and the large number of vendor booths was surprising even to Eunice. She spied everything from quilts to homemade peanut butter to turkey calls. The mood was jolly. The crowds were out. And the weather couldn't have been better if they'd special ordered it.

She made her way to Gideon's office and knocked lightly on the door frame. When he glanced up, she said, "I'm surprised you're in here. Suspected I'd have to search the grounds for you."

"Eunice! Perfect timing. I still need you in the Backyard Barnyard. Think you can handle it?"

"Animals and a barn? *Ya.* I can handle it."

"You're the best." His phone rang at the same time that another auctioneer appeared at his door.

Eunice offered a wave, then rushed off in the direction of the animal barn which acted as a sort of petting zoo. They usually kept a few sheep, some ponies, goats, rabbits and a cow. Eunice hurried into the small office, switched the sign from *Closed* to *Open* and was relieved to see two girls from her church show up.

"We usually help on the weekends, but Gideon asked us to work extra hours for the festival." Elizabeth Schrock was eighteen years old, dark-haired and pretty. She'd moved here after Zeb had moved away, so she probably didn't know him. Eunice could make an introduction.

Why was she thinking about Zeb's dating life?

She needed to focus on the job at hand.

Hannah Glick was also young, eligible and attractive— though in a more studious way. She wore blue-rimmed glasses and always carried a book in her apron pocket. "Is everything okay, Eunice?"

"*Ya.* Of course."

"We didn't know what to do when we saw the *Back in a Moment* sign."

"I'm going to help out today. Can you two handle the guests if I start sending them through?"

"*Ya.* No problem."

"I'll take care of the pony rides," Hannah said.

"And I'll walk them through the various animal pens." Elizabeth smiled.

Eunice felt instantly relieved. They were a team. They'd make this work.

No sooner had they settled on the details of their shift, than a family of five *Englischers* showed up asking if their children could pet the sheep. The morning flew by, and Eunice was surprised when Noah showed up to give her a late lunch break.

"I thought you were in charge of renovations."

"No projects this week." He grinned. "According to Amos it's all hands…"

"On deck," Eunice said.

"Grab some lunch and don't come back for at least an hour. You've earned a break." He sank into her chair. "Looks pretty quiet here."

"Just wait until the guests return from their lunch. Earlier this morning, we had a line for the pony rides that stretched around the barn. Then everyone realized they were hungry, and this entire area emptied out."

"Ah. Makes sense. Enjoy your lunch."

She waved goodbye and hurried away. It actually felt good to be out and about. Two young *Englisch* women walked past, each pushing a baby stroller. An older Amish couple stopped to admire the fresh vegetables on display in a booth.

Perhaps this was what would soothe the restlessness that plagued her. It could be as simple as needing to get out of the barn. She definitely felt more comfortable here than in a yarn shop—though she had survived her first knitting lesson the week before. Still, if the yarn gig didn't work, maybe she should ask her *dat* if he had an opening at the market she could fill.

She shook her head at that thought.

Must be the hunger talking.

She'd finished a burger and shake and was making her way back a bit more slowly to the barnyard since she still had twenty minutes left when she practically ran into Zeb and Josh. He was trying to hurry his son along. Josh wasn't having it. He sat down in the middle of the walking path and pulled off his shoe, shaking out a small pile of dirt.

"Problem?" she asked.

"We were ahead of time, but then Josh had a minor meltdown over lunch, and now—" He waved toward his son who was quite focused on pulling off his sock. "I have a tour starting in ten minutes on the other side of the market and my son woke up in an uncooperative m-o-o-d."

"There's something in my sock," Josh explained, turning it inside out and shaking it for good measure.

"We need to hurry, son."

"I don't want to hurry. Why do you have to go on a dumb ol' tour, anyway?"

Eunice and Zeb shared a look, then Zeb raised both hands in surrender. Eunice almost laughed.

"Hey. I thought you were coming to the barnyard to help me this afternoon. I could sure use your help with the sheep and ponies and the cow." Eunice realized she was laying it on a little thick, but they needed to get this parade on the move.

Zeb was wearing his perpetually worried expression, but Josh studied her in complete surprise. His I'm-More-Stubborn-Than-You look had all but disappeared.

"Where are you going, Eunice?"

"Barn. Animals. Didn't your *dat* tell you about this?"

"I did, but apparently he wasn't listening."

"Yes!" Josh hurriedly pulled his shoe back on, then stared at the sock still in his hand as if he wasn't sure what to do with it.

"I'll hold that for you." She accepted the sock and folded it in half. Kids' socks were so small, as was Josh's hand which he slipped into hers.

"Can I really go with you?"

"Absolutely. Your *dat* and I worked out the details yesterday."

Zeb looked as his son, checked his watch, then rubbed a hand up and down his jawline.

"Problem?" Eunice asked.

"*Nein.* Nothing like that. You two have a *gut* time with the animals."

"Aye-aye, Captain," Eunice said. "We will have a *gut* time, and we'll see to the animals."

Zeb took the sock from her hand and gave it to his son. "Put that back on. Not over your shoe, son."

Then he turned his back so that Josh wouldn't be privy to what he was about to say.

"Remember to watch him closely. Five-year-olds can find trouble like bees find a flower."

"Uh-huh."

"Don't let him talk you into a bunch of sweets either. That just makes him more energetic, which you don't want."

"You know, Zeb, this is my third week babysitting Josh. Plus, I have two nieces nearly his age. I've been around children before."

"*Ya*, well. Being in charge of a child is very different

from being around a child." He started to walk away, then turned back.

"Danki," he said to Eunice, then crouched in front of his son. "Do what Eunice says."

"Okay."

"Mind your manners."

"I will."

"I'll be back in a couple hours."

"Ten-four."

Eunice and Josh stood watching Zeb as he disappeared into the crowd.

"He's a worrywart," Josh said.

"Where did you learn that word?"

"Mammi."

"Ya?"

"Yup. Say, Eunice, is there really a cow where you're working? Could I ride it? Do you think that sheep can be taught to roll over? And I was wondering, if I could find a snake, would you like to show it to the *Englischers*?"

Eunice didn't bother answering.

Josh's attention reminded her of a Ferris wheel she'd ridden when she was a child. One minute you're looking at one thing and having big thoughts about it. The next minute, you're looking at a completely different thing, and your thoughts shift. She had noticed that Josh's thoughts did a lot of jumping from one thing to another, and the boy's abundance of energy was testament to that.

He'd do great in the Backyard Barnyard.

It would be like being home with his *dat* and *onkel*.

Zeb's words of caution rang in her ears, but she dismissed his warning. He reiterated his concerns every day. She was becoming immune to his words of caution, and she'd been around kids way more than he realized. She helped watch children at sew-ins, occasionally volunteered at the school when they were in a real bind for a substitute teacher and had even babysat each of her nieces and nephews. She hadn't lost a single kid yet.

She and Josh would be fine.

What could possibly go wrong?

Zeb was finishing up with his third Behind the Scenes Market Tour when he noticed Gideon lurking near the back of the crowd. Zeb handed an Amish farms tour map to the *Englischer* who had asked about home businesses and quilt gardens. She thanked him and walked away, which was when Gideon moved forward.

"Don't panic," he said, then clarified that with, "Sorry, not a great way to start."

"What's wrong?"

"Josh is fine."

"Why wouldn't he be fine?"

"He had a little fall, but the market's medic has already checked him out and—"

"You called the medic?" Zeb looked around, as if he'd forgotten his horse and buggy or perhaps his first aid kit, then turned back to Gideon. "Where is he? Is he in the hospital?"

"*Nein.* He's fine, Zeb."

"If he's fine, you wouldn't be here."

"Okay. Take a deep breath." Gideon moved directly in front of him, effectively blocking his view. "Seriously. Calm down before you see him or you'll scare the kid to death."

"Right. Okay. *Ya.* You're right." He pulled a breath deep into his lungs then let it go. Again. And then a third time— just as the counselor had taught him after Suzanne died, when he'd sometimes found himself dizzy with grief.

"Better?"

"Ya."

"Let's go then."

As they walked toward the barn, Gideon explained what had happened. Apparently Josh had decided to climb onto the cow, though Eunice and the girls working there had warned him not to do so.

"He's a hardheaded child," Zeb admitted.

"He managed to get on the cow's back, but then of course she moved, knocking him off. When he fell he hit his head on the ground."

"Stitches?"

"Nope. Just a large goose egg."

He could see the barn now, and it was all Zeb could do not to push through the crowd and sprint the rest of the way.

"Thanks for coming to get me."

"Of course. And Zeb…" Gideon waited until Zeb stopped and turned toward him. "Go easy on Eunice. She feels really bad that it happened on her watch."

Eunice!

He knew that he shouldn't leave Josh with her. She'd never had a child. She knew nothing about children, and when he'd tried to warn her, she'd basically blown him off. Just because she'd had a few weeks of watching him on her home turf, didn't mean she was ready to watch him in public.

Still, she was family to Gideon. Zeb had enough presence of mind to nod and hope that Gideon took that as agreement.

He hurried to the entrance of the barn. Several guests were standing in line, waiting for their turn to go through the animal pens. Eunice was working at the little office's window, taking money and handing out maps. And Josh was sitting on a chair beside her, holding an ice pack to his head and grinning broadly.

"Dat!" He hopped up, but Eunice put a hand on his shoulder, leaned down and whispered something to him.

The boy nodded emphatically. "Forgot. I'm not supposed to run any more today. Gotta give the bump time to go down."

The *Englischers* moved off and Zeb walked into the office, squatting in front of his son. He pulled away the ice pack and saw the goose egg above his son's right eye. Fear threatened to choke him and his pulse began to race. He tried not to picture his son with only one good eye, his son bleeding and on the ground, his son at the hospital. He tried, but all of those things flashed through his mind.

Suddenly, he realized Josh was watching him and waiting. He attempted a smile. "You're okay?"

"Ya. See this sticker?" He pointed to a sticker that said *I'm a Star.* "Got it because I didn't even cry. Well, not much. I mean at first, when I hit the ground, I did cry, but then when Eunice told me to settle down, I did."

"You told him what?" He turned to Eunice, unable to believe what he was hearing. A child falls off a cow, which he shouldn't have been allowed on in the first place, nearly busts open his noggin, and she tells him to settle down?

"We had a bit of theatrics at first," she admitted. "But Josh calmed down, and the medic came, and he was a real champ."

Eunice grinned at Josh.

Josh grinned at Eunice.

Zeb feared his head might explode. "I'm proud of you, buddy. Can you stay here while Eunice and I have a private talk?"

"Sure, *Dat.* I know all about your private talks. They're usually kind of boring. Sorry. Probably shouldn't have said that." He zipped his mouth shut, then pushed the ice pack back on his bump.

Zeb jerked his head to the right.

Gideon, who was still waiting outside the office said, "I'll just…take over here for a few minutes."

Somehow Zeb managed to hold in his anger until they were at the far end of the pony grazing area. Then he turned on Eunice with the fury of a summer storm. "What were you thinking?"

"What do you mean, what was I thinking?"

"How could you allow him on a cow?"

"I didn't allow him on a cow. In fact, I specifically told him *not* to get on the cow. But I turned around, and next thing I knew there was screaming that was loud enough to alert *Englischers* for miles."

"He was screaming?"

Eunice put her hands on her hips and stared at the ground. Finally she looked up and said, "He was crying loudly. More loudly than he needed to."

"More loudly than he—" Once again, Zeb feared that his anger would win total control over what he was about to say. He stuffed his feelings down, made sure he had complete control over his emotions, then faced Eunice. "You should have watched him more closely."

"You're kidding."

"No. I'm not."

"You can't watch a child every minute of every day."

"I shouldn't have left him with you. I should have followed my instincts. I knew you weren't ready."

"Wait." Her eyes had widened, and she was clutching her hands at her side. "Are you actually saying this is *my* fault?"

"Yes, it's your fault. It's certainly not Josh's fault." And then his left arm began to shake—another physical display of stress that took him back to the days immediately following Suzanne's death. He clamped it to his side, hoping Eunice hadn't noticed.

"Look, Zeb. I'm sorry that Josh has a bump on his head. But kids get bumps on their head. It's not a big deal."

"You don't understand." A feeling of solid ice came over him. "How could you? No child of your own. No idea what it's like to be responsible for someone else…to be the only one responsible. You're right about one thing. This isn't your fault completely. It's my fault. I shouldn't have left him with you."

"I'm sorry you feel that way, but just maybe this isn't my fault or your fault. Maybe it's Josh's fault because he needs to learn to mind his elders. And that's normal, Zeb. That's how kids learn. They get bumps and bruises and then they learn not to do a thing—like not to climb on the backs of cows."

But Zeb wasn't listening.

Oh, he could hear her as he walked away, but he wasn't really listening to a word she said. Because Eunice Yoder had no idea what she was talking about.

He knew what it meant to be a father.

And today was one more instance of how he'd managed to fail even at that. He could accept failure, but he wouldn't be repeating this mistake. He wouldn't leave his son with Eunice Yoder again. That was nonnegotiable.

Next time he needed a babysitter—which would be tomorrow, he'd trust one of the *youngies* his *mamm* had suggested. Even a teenager could do a better job than Eunice Yoder. He almost pitied the guy who finally married her, but he was very grateful that she wasn't his problem. He had all the problems he could handle. He did not need to add Eunice to that list.

Chapter Seven

$\sim$

Zeb had apparently picked the wrong day to fire his child-care provider. He could not find a replacement for Eunice, and he had another tour to host the next day. Plus the following week they were expanding to tours that began and ended at the market, but included several Amish businesses at their homes. He'd be gone even longer hours. He needed someone dependable to watch Josh.

He spent over an hour at the phone booth as Josh played outside it in the dirt. Every single person he called turned him down.

They had jobs in town.

They had plans for the weekend.

They had plans every weekday and weekend.

They were working at the market.

The list of excuses grew as long as the list of numbers he dialed. There were a few octogenarians that he hadn't tried, but one look outside the phone booth—one glimpse of Joshua painting an outline around the buggy with mud—and he tossed the idea of an eighty-year-old watching him right out the window.

Where had the boy found mud? It hadn't rained in a week. Then Zeb saw the water spigot, meant for watering horses, and beneath that a plastic red cup someone had left behind. Mystery solved.

Josh saw his father walking toward him and froze, mid mud painting. "Am I in trouble?"

"Should you be?"

Josh glanced down at his clothes—dark blue pants, white shirt, suspenders—all a muddy brown. "Well, we are farmers, and farmers do work in the dirt."

"Indeed, they do."

Instead of reprimanding him for adding to the list of chores needing to be done—those mud stains were going to require soaking—Zeb walked over to the horse and leaned his forehead against hers.

Soon he felt a small, slightly dirty, kind of gritty hand slip into his.

"What's wrong, *Dat*?"

Zeb took in a deep breath. Time to act like an adult. Time to once again pretend that he had a solution for every problem. "Nothing, son. Nothing at all."

Josh cocked his head and said, "Honesty, please."

It was something that Zeb had said to his son several times a week in the last year.

The lamp simply *fell* off the table? "Honesty, please."

The last three cookies *disappeared*? "Honesty, please."

Someone ran across the garden rows, burying a few of the plants with a size four shoe? "Honesty, please."

So, when Josh said those same words back to him, Zeb couldn't help smiling...and being honest. "Guess it's you and me, son. Couldn't find anyone else for you to stay with while I give tours."

"That's not such a bad thing."

"But I have to go to work."

"Why can't I just go to Eunice's?" Zeb touched the bump on his forehead. "Because of this?"

"Well, not exactly. I think we need someone who has more experience babysitting five-year-old boys."

"Huh. But I liked staying with Eunice."

"I know you did."

"She's nice."

"Yup."

"And she knows how to fix stuff."

"Indeed."

Josh sighed and slapped his hands together, attempting to dislodge the dried mud. "Guess I could go with you."

"I guess you could." Zeb didn't think it was a good solution, but it was the only one he had at the moment. Even his own brother had plans for the following day.

They went home where he tended to the horse, threw together sandwiches for dinner, made sure Joshua had a bath and put the boy's clothes in a bucket to soak the mud off them. By the time he was reading Josh his bedtime story, Zeb's own eyes were drifting shut same as his son's. He woke up an hour later with a crick in his neck and an even worse attitude than he'd had before.

As he passed through the living room to turn out the light in the kitchen, he noticed how disheveled everything was. Damp bath towel lying across the back of the sofa. Books and crayons scattered across the living room floor. Dirty dishes still on the table. Zeb ignored it all and trudged down the hall to his bedroom which took him past his brother's open door.

His brother.

Still out at…how could it only be nine o'clock? It felt like at least midnight. When had he become that guy who fell asleep before nine in the evening? Why did he feel so old? Why was he perpetually exhausted?

He trudged to his room, managed to brush his teeth and then collapsed onto his bed. But as tired as he was, his mind insisted on replaying the day's events.

Gideon telling him to take a breath.

Josh holding an ice pack to his head.

Eunice insisting *you can't watch a child every minute of every day.*

How he had reacted in anger.

He couldn't remember exactly what he'd said to her, but it hadn't been kind. This parenting gig was so much harder than he'd ever imagined it could be. Of course, he'd never imagined doing it alone. He was tired and frustrated and grasping at straws, and he'd taken all of those things out on Eunice.

Rolling over, he raised up, punched his pillow, then settled back down. "She should have watched him closer," he muttered to no one. Because no one was there. He was going to have to deal with this particular situation—with his life—entirely on his own.

He slept fitfully and woke early the next morning. Cleaned up the house. Washed and hung a load of laundry. Made breakfast. By the time Samuel and Josh walked into the kitchen, Zeb had already been up for three hours. He casually glanced at his son's head. The bump was nearly gone. Still visible but only if you knew to look for it.

Maybe it hadn't been as bad as he'd thought.

Maybe he'd overreacted.

Samuel raised an eyebrow as he glanced around the kitchen. "Why are you up with the birds?"

"Chickens," Josh said. "He's up with the chickens."

"Needed to tidy up around here. What time did you get in?"

"I don't know." Samuel yawned as he poured himself a cup of coffee. "Late. Why? Do I have a curfew?"

"What's a curfew?" Josh was attempting to layer his eggs on top of his bacon and eat it like a sandwich.

"Stop playing with your food, son."

"Why can't I have cereal?"

"Because cereal isn't as healthy as eggs."

"I know what you mean, little man. I wouldn't mind some Apple Jacks, myself." Samuel high-fived Josh.

Zeb wanted to hold on to his irritation at his *bruder*, but he needed to conserve his energy. He stared longingly at the coffeepot on the stove. Did he dare to drink another cup? He'd already had three, and he could feel the blood pulsing through his veins. He shook his head and poured himself a glass of water from the pitcher they kept in the fridge.

The rest of the meal passed in silence, for which Zeb was very grateful. He'd woken with a dull throbbing at the base of his neck. Funny that his son was the one with the injury, but he was the one with the pain. He supposed that described parenthood pretty well.

Josh asked to be excused, set his dishes in the sink, then dashed outside.

"Stay out of the dirt," Zeb called after him. "And don't even think about getting those clothes dirty."

Samuel studied him over his second cup of coffee.

Zeb stared back at his *bruder*, wondering what he could say to explain the depth of his misery. Looking at Samuel was very much like looking in a mirror, except Samuel was three years older, a hair taller and a little thinner. Plus, he had that perpetual grin on his face. He finally settled for simply asking, "What?"

"I didn't say anything."

"But you wanted to. Just say it."

"I was just wondering what you're so out of sorts about."

Samuel finished the coffee and reached for the last piece of bacon.

"Didn't say I was out of sorts."

"Didn't have to."

Zeb should have kept quiet. He'd woken that morning certain that in order to survive he had to get better control of his emotions. He'd even taken five minutes to page through his Bible. His *mamm* had given him a bookmark with a daily reading guide for Christmas the year before. He hadn't used it much, but he did this morning.

Colossians chapter 4, verse 6, read, "Let your speech be always with grace…"

Yeah. His words the day before had been a lot of things but full of grace they were not. He'd vowed to do better. He'd even bowed his head and prayed that *Gotte* would help him do better. And now this. Something in his brother's casual demeanor and amused expression pushed all the wrong buttons.

"Any chance you noticed the bump on my son's head?"

"I noticed."

"Did you even think to ask about it?"

"Didn't have to ask, Zeb. Heard all of the details last night."

"From whom?"

Samuel waved away that question. "He fell off a cow. He's okay. What's the big deal?"

"The big deal is that Eunice was supposed to be watching him."

"And?"

"And she did a terrible job."

"Because he crawled on the back of the cow and then fell off?"

"Now you sound like her."

"Hmm. Look." Samuel yawned, rubbed his hands over his face, then picked up the coffee cup, stared into it and finally set it back down on the table. "I heard you fired Eunice, which personally I think is unfair. But the bigger question, the one that probably has you in such a sour mood, is what are you going to do with Joshua when you go to work today?"

"Any chance that you—"

"Nope."

"Nope?" Zeb had already known the answer was going to be no. His *bruder* worked every Friday, and he went out every Friday night. He went out most nights.

"I work," Samuel said. "And then I have a date. You remember dates, right?"

Zeb bit back his retort. "I don't need a sitter. I'm taking him with me." It certainly sounded doable when he said it with confidence.

"Did you ask Amos about that?"

"I did not. Josh will be fine. The tour group won't even know he's there."

At least that's the way he envisioned it in his head.

But when had life turned out like he'd envisioned it? He pushed that particular thought away, plastered on a smile so Samuel wouldn't think he was sour and stood to clean the breakfast dishes. One thing he knew for certain. A single dad's work was never done.

Eunice had spoken with *Dat* at dinner the night before. She'd told him about Josh's accident and about Zeb firing her as Josh's babysitter. Her father had been uncharacteristically quiet. He'd basically nodded, made sympathetic noises, then asked if there was any leftover pumpkin bread that he could have for dessert. She could barely believe it. He was letting the whole topic slide.

The next morning, she realized that wasn't the case.

As soon as she sat down for breakfast—it was his morning to cook—she knew something was up. He'd scrambled eggs and made toast. Most mornings they settled for oatmeal.

"I've been thinking about your predicament," he said.

She swallowed the first bite of eggs, then responded with, "You have?"

"I might have a solution."

"Uh-oh."

Amos laughed, slathered strawberry preserves made by one of her *schweschdern* onto his toast, took a giant bite, chewed and swallowed. "You still need another part-time job."

"Or a beau."

He froze with his hand on his coffee cup, met her eyes and smiled. "You had me there for a minute."

"Did I?"

"Thought maybe you'd met someone."

"Since I went to bed last night?"

"Let's move on. You need another part-time job, and Zeb needs another stop on his tour."

"Wait. What? I thought the tours were at the market."

"They have been. That's how we started, but beginning next week they'll expand to visit places off-site."

"Such as…"

"They'll go to Naomi Schwartz's home and view her sewing business."

Naomi was a real whiz with a sewing needle and a pedal machine. She had two sets of twins, managed to make all of her children's clothes and still had time to make items that she sold to *Englischers*.

Amos had sat back and was staring across the room. Eunice knew he was envisioning the tour route, seeing how it would play out. Seeing the smiles on the tourists' faces.

"Then Jess Hochstetler's farm to learn about how we raise animals and grow crops."

"Is that different from how *Englischers* do such things?"

"It is, maybe more than you realize. After that, Zeb will guide them to Martha Lapp's to see her quilting. All this is done with an *Englisch* driver."

"Which one?" Eunice was stalling. She did not like the direction this conversation was going.

"Old Tom, Jocelyn and Martin. Each will take one day of the week."

They were the three best drivers in their community— dependable, friendly, with large, comfy vehicles. They were who Eunice would have picked.

"The last stop was supposed to be a walk-through of Esmerelda's little loom shop including a chance to buy any of her rugs, followed by tea."

"Wow. Sounds like you had this planned down to the last buggy ride. Wait. Are there buggy rides?"

Amos laughed. "Back at the market, guests will have a chance to climb up into a buggy and ride around the small downtown area."

"Doesn't someone else already do those sorts of tours around Shipshe?"

"Indeed. I talked to the guy—a swell fellow who lives over in Goshen and is a Mennonite. He said he's had to turn folks away. Every tour is full. That's what gave me the idea."

"Hmm." Eunice still had a bad feeling about where her *dat* was going with this. How could she possibly help provide a stop on Zeb's tours? Plus, there was the fact that she was probably the last person Zeb Mast wanted to see at the moment.

"Sadly, Esmerelda King has broken her ankle. There's no way she can be a stop on the tour now. You know she has that large loom she makes rugs on."

"I'm aware. We have one in our living room."

"She'll be going to stay with her *schweschder* in Middlebury for at least six weeks, maybe longer."

"So, no loom stop on the tour."

"No loom stop."

Eunice pushed her plate and coffee out of the way, placed both hands on the table—one over the other, and voiced the question she wasn't sure we wanted to know the answer to. "What does Esmerelda's terrible accident have to do with me?"

"You could take her place."

"I'm not following."

"On the tour."

"Still not following. I don't sew or quilt or farm or loom."

Amos waved toward the barn. "You could show them your gizmos. How we integrate solar power into our simple life. That sort of thing."

Now she sat back and crossed her arms. "Assuming Zeb would want me on his tour, which at the moment is a mighty big assumption, how much did Esmerelda make?"

"Well, the total proceeds are divided by the four stops on the tour, the tour guide and the driver. Tips are split, as well. Fifteen percent each for the four tour stops. Twenty percent for the driver and the tour guide—since they're with the group the entire time."

"What about the market? Don't you get a cut?"

"For the tours that stay on the market, yes. I split that money with Zeb. But for the tours that are off the property, I don't."

"And how much do you figure that fifteen percent will come to...roughly?"

Amos named a figure that caused Eunice to whistle. "Seriously?"

"*Ya.* Tours bring in *gut* money. *Englischers* enjoy a look behind the scenes, peering into the belly of the ship, so to speak."

She squinted at him.

"I think you'd be a *wunderbaar* addition to the tour."

"You do?" She didn't have to fake a look of surprise. She was surprised. Flummoxed.

"Ya."

"But…" She swallowed, glanced left and right, then finally looked directly at her father. "I always thought you were a little embarrassed by what I do."

"Nein. I was never embarrassed."

Those words sat between them for a long moment.

"Okay." She blinked back tears, caused not just by his words, but also because of the tender expression on his face. Her father wasn't embarrassed by her? Was it possible that he was even proud of her? She'd never even considered it. She'd stayed as far away from that question as possible.

Blinking rapidly, she fiddled with her coffee cup until she had her emotions under control. Crying at breakfast was never a productive way to start the day. "Okay. But what about Josh? I mean, if I'm not watching Josh, and assuming Zeb hasn't found anyone else, he might have to stop doing the tours. At least until he works out childcare."

"Well, I've been thinking about that. I might have a solution."

Of course he did. He hadn't been quietly accepting the situation the night before. He'd been plotting the next turn of events.

Though the amount of money he'd quoted could go a long way toward Eunice's financial independence. And she *was* proud of the work she did in the barn. She missed it, actually. To be able to show that side of Amish life to guests, to show them a nontraditional Amish woman. That idea appealed to her.

The fly in the ointment was that she'd be working with Zeb. And Zebedee Mast was not happy with her at the moment. She wasn't particularly happy with him either.

Still, to be able to do the work she was good at, the work she was confident with, for even part of the week was a lovely idea. It outweighed any reservations she might have about Zeb. Which was why she turned to her *dat* and said, "Explain it to me."

"Simple, really. Your *schweschder*, Becca, would watch Josh and serve the refreshments at the end of the tour. It would be good if you shared some of what you make with her."

"Of course. But does Becca really have the time and energy to do that? With an almost four-year-old and a seven-month-old baby?"

She thought *Dat* would brush off that particular concern. Would wave away any questions. Obviously, he'd already talked to Becca and Gideon, and they had agreed. Eunice was aware that she didn't need to know the details. But the fact that he nodded slowly and explained it to her, that meant a lot. It made her feel as if she was another adult in the family.

"Becca is quite busy with the children, but she also misses her mission work. This wouldn't be that. She understands that tourists aren't the mission field. However, she and Gideon have prayed on this, and she thinks she can make a difference. Offering refreshment is a little thing, but isn't it the essence of what we're called to do? Be the hands of Christ, wherever and whenever possible?"

Eunice nodded.

"As for watching Josh, he will play well with little Mary. That's our hope, anyway."

She should have guessed that Becca had an altruistic reason for pitching in. Still, it could work. They could do this, and it would be good to be involved in something as a family. Well, a family plus Zeb and Josh. It stung a little that Zeb didn't trust her with his son. A part of Eunice was hurt that he had judged her so harshly, that he had so little faith in her. Not that she had romantic feelings toward him, but rejection of any type hurt.

Another part of her realized that Zeb was very much still in the throes of grief over losing his wife.

He couldn't see past what he'd lost. Maybe he didn't want to. Maybe he didn't know how. The question was whether he'd ever find his way out from that dark place. She realized in that moment that she was worried about him. They'd been friends as long as she could remember. She didn't want to see him hurting and angry. She didn't want to see him struggling to raise his son alone. If he was successful with the tours, he'd be one step closer to purchasing his parents' farm. With the financial pressure eased, perhaps he would start dating a woman in their congregation.

She could help by agreeing to be a stop on his tour.

It was a little thing.

"It's a deal," she said with a nod that caused her *dat* to stand and pull her into a hug. They weren't a family that often showed their affections with hugs and such, but she needed that contact this morning. She took in the smell of him and understood how much her father meant to her. She depended a lot on him, and perhaps it was time that she become more independent. Maybe her father had been right all along. It was time to move forward with her life.

Chapter Eight

~

Zeb's day couldn't have gone much worse. He and Josh walked out to the parking area, neither saying much. It had been that kind of day. Even his young, energetic son was silent.

Ben Gold was in charge of pasturing the horses, caring for them, then helping workers to harness them when it was time to go. But Ben wasn't who met Zeb at his buggy. Instead, Amos had fetched Beauty and was guiding her out of the pasture.

"Amos."

"Afternoon, Zeb. Fine mare you have here."

"*Ya*. My parents bought her four years ago, while I was in Lancaster."

Beauty and the buggy were given to Zeb and Samuel when his parents moved. It wasn't as if they could ship a horse, and they understood that both sons were working hard to find a way to purchase the farm. He was grateful for the mare. She had a gentle and patient nature. Something Zeb realized he might be able to learn from the horse.

"How are you doing, young Josh?"

"Not so good." Josh blew out a big breath, causing his lips to make a propeller sound. "Been in trouble most of the afternoon."

"Ah."

"We had rather a rough day," Zeb admitted.

Amos seemed to consider that, then nodded as he patted Beauty's neck.

"God won't lead you where His grace can't keep you," Amos said, then winked at Josh. "Sounds like something one of my *doschdern* might stitch onto a pillow case, but I believe it to be true."

"Sure. That makes sense." Zeb had a bad feeling though.

Why was Amos working parking detail? Had one of the guests complained about the day's tour? Was he about to be fired? He wasn't sure he wanted to make a career out of being a tour guide but at this moment in time, he needed this job.

As if reading his thoughts, Amos said, "I was wondering if we could talk for a moment."

"Of course. Josh, why don't you go and play for a few minutes. And—"

"Be careful. I know." The boy walked away, his head down as if he was expecting to be hollered at.

Zeb glanced up at Amos. The man was a fair boss, and he'd raised five daughters on his own. Maybe he could offer some advice because Zeb was completely out of ideas.

"Did you hear about Esmerelda's accident?" Amos asked.

"*Nein.* What happened?"

"Tripped over a garden hose. Broke her ankle pretty badly. She'll be going to live with her *schweschder* in Middlebury until it heals."

"So, she's off the tour."

"I'm afraid so."

Jiminy Cricket. The day just continued to get worse. "What does that mean as far as the tour?"

"I think we definitely do need a fourth stop."

"Sure. *Ya.* I agree."

"I've talked to Becca and Eunice."

"About—" Zeb stopped there because he couldn't for the life of him think of anything that Becca and Eunice would have to do with his tours.

A smile tugged at the corners of Amos's mouth. "I spoke to Eunice about being the fourth stop on the tour."

"I don't understand."

"Eunice is quite good at repairing small machines. It might be interesting for the tour group to see an Amish woman in a less than traditional role."

Zeb shook his head. Not because he disagreed. But because he couldn't imagine Eunice wanting to have anything to do with him after the brusque way he'd spoken to her. And even if she had said yes, which apparently she had, there was still the issue of childcare.

"I guess you heard about Josh's accident yesterday."

"*Ya*. How's he feeling?"

"Fine. Just fine. But I'm going to be honest with you, Amos. I tried taking Josh with me on the tour today, and it didn't go well. In fact, I thought you might be about to fire me."

"I wouldn't do that, Zeb."

An unexpected release of tension caused him to feel momentarily lightheaded. Had he even eaten lunch? Or breakfast? He pulled his attention back to the man standing in front of him. "Okay. That's good to know. But today's tour here at the market was a disaster. When we went into the canteen's kitchen, Josh pulled an entire platter of cookies down on the floor, burning his finger in the process."

"I noticed the bandage on his finger."

"*Ya*. Fortunately, it wasn't bad. But before that we'd gone to the Backyard Barnyard, and this time instead of falling off a cow, he let out the sheep. Took the girls working there a full half hour to round them back up."

The day's misadventures came spilling out of Zeb. On one level, he realized he might look back and laugh at this day when Josh was grown with *kinder* of his own. But today? Today, it just felt as if everything had gone wrong. As if he hadn't done enough to make sure things went right.

"There's more. At the RV park, he tripped over someone's sewer hose, then he fell on the ground into the liquid that was spilling out of the hose. The mess was on Josh, spread out over the guy's camping area, everywhere."

"That would explain his pants and the smell."

"I'm doing it all wrong, Amos." Zeb took Beauty's lead and walked her to his buggy.

He needed to be doing something. He couldn't look at Amos as he confessed his shortcomings. "I'm short-tempered, exhausted all the time and I am constantly behind on something. I thought being a farmer was hard, but…"

He stopped talking then.

He simply could not voice the fact that he felt like an abject failure.

Amos had followed him to the buggy. Now he helped to harness Beauty, then nodded toward Josh who was dashing back and forth under the trees trying to catch leaves as they fell. "He's a fine child, Zeb. And I imagine you are doing a *gut* job."

"How could you possibly say that?"

"Because he's happy. He's happy chasing leaves." Amos grinned broadly and there was no doubt that he meant what he said. Then his expression sobered a bit. "That's not true of all children in this life. It's not even true of all children in this town. The fact that he is happy, it speaks to the fact that he knows you love him and care for him."

It couldn't be that simple. Zeb appreciated Amos trying to cheer him up, but it really could not be that simple.

"I know a little about being a single *dat*. It's difficult. I wouldn't lie and tell you that it's easy. But it is worth it. Seeing our children grow into well-balanced, healthy adults..." Amos's voice had taken on a softer tone, and his gaze was focused on the horizon—as if he were looking into the past rather than across the parking area. "It's worth everything we go through."

Zeb patted the mare, then stood with his back against the buggy, staring at his son. He stood beside Amos and tried to believe the wisdom his boss was sharing. Then he remembered the current pressing problem. "I still don't have any childcare," he admitted.

"I might have an idea that will help with that."

Zeb drove home ten minutes later. He wasn't convinced that Amos's solution would work, but it had to be better than his own failed attempt at solving the problem. Because if it wasn't, he wasn't sure what his next step would be.

Eunice would have liked to have avoided Zeb until their first tour the following week. She was still incensed that he'd fired her as a childcare provider. Honestly, she thought he'd come back apologizing and begging her to give him one more chance. That didn't happen. Instead, her *dat* had brokered the deal where Becca was watching Josh.

But it was hard to avoid someone during church. Even harder to stay out of their way at the luncheon afterward.

"Just go over and talk to him," Becca advised.

"No."

"Why?"

They were both working the dessert table. Zeb had actually bypassed the sweets so that he wouldn't have to face her. She thought that was amazing. The guy had a sweet tooth, but it seemed the pull of double chocolate cake wasn't enough to overcome his embarrassment.

"Why should I? He's the one in the wrong."

"Oh, Eunice."

Eunice pinned her with a stare, causing Becca to raise her hands in surrender, then push the strawberry pie to the front of the table. Sighing, Becca moved the platter of oatmeal cookies to the right and the brownie bars to the left. Then switched them back again.

"Just say it."

Becca smiled gently. "But you don't want me to."

"Better than you taking it out on the desserts."

Becca looked up at her, suddenly serious, and Eunice felt bad for causing such concern on her *schweschder*'s face. She was always concerning her family. It seemed that everything she did, every decision she made, resulted in someone feeling the need to explain why it had been wrong.

Which wasn't true.

She knew it wasn't true. She wasn't always wrong. But she felt *off* today. She felt as if she'd rolled out of the wrong side of the bed, but her bed was positioned against a wall so that wasn't even possible. "I'm just in a bad mood. Didn't sleep well."

"Why?"

"Because I was arguing with Zeb in my head. I'll have you know, I won every single time."

Everyone had been through the line except for the women and girls working at the food tables. Becca tugged on Eunice's arm and nodded toward the path that circled the Glicks' small pond.

"Aren't you hungry?" Eunice asked.

"It'll still be here. Let's walk."

So they did, and by the time they were halfway around

the pond, some of the restless energy had drained out of her. They sat in the grass and watched the group of families on the opposite side of the water. She could just make out Zeb and Josh, sitting with the older people. Why would he sit with the older people? This was his chance to let Josh be around children his own age.

"Tell me what you're thinking."

"Right now? Right now I'm thinking that Zeb should be sitting with people his own age."

"Ah."

"Ah, what?"

"Maybe he's uncomfortable with people his own age."

"Because—"

"Because most of them are married, and he's not."

Ugh. Eunice hated it when Becca looked at the compassionate side of things. It always made her feel like such a snake.

"You think he should have moved on."

"I don't know," Eunice hedged. "Maybe. Okay, yes. I do. It's time to put his son first."

"Probably an easier thing to say than do, and maybe—in his mind—he is putting Josh first."

"I guess." Eunice circled her arms around her knees. It felt childish, but it also felt comforting. "Why can't he just be Zeb? The Zeb I grew up with. Why does he have to be so ornery and cranky all the time?"

"Perhaps what you're calling orneriness and crankiness is simply grief."

"Maybe so."

"And grief sometimes feels like fear."

Eunice turned her head so that her cheek was rested against her knees but her gaze was on Becca. "Amish proverb?"

"C.S. Lewis."

"Oh, I remember that book about the lion. What was his name?"

"Aslan, but we're sliding away from the point here."

"Is the point that Zeb is afraid?"

"It's a possibility."

"Of what?"

Becca pulled Eunice to her feet, looped her arm through her *schweschder*'s and started walking them the rest of the way around the pond. Toward the food tables. Toward the people. Toward Zeb.

"Maybe everything."

"Huh?"

"Maybe Zeb's afraid of everything. Grief can color your world, Eunice. When I worked with Mennonite Disaster Services, people were very grateful for the help that we offered. But they were still grieving. It wasn't always sunshine and roses."

"Ada would have said sunshine and ponies."

"Probably." Becca squeezed her arm. "My point is that people need time to heal after a terrible loss."

"How much time?"

"Depends on the person."

Eunice realized as they finished the walk and she filled her plate with food that she didn't want to let go of her anger toward Zeb. Her certainty, her self-righteousness was like a sweater that she'd grown very comfortable wearing.

But it wasn't their way.

Becca had reminded her of that though she hadn't said those exact words. The commandment to love one another often went unsaid, though it was very important in the way they tried to live like Christ. Holding a grudge, being angry, harboring ill will was not their way. They were called to love.

Hadn't the sermon they'd just heard been on that very thing? *Love your neighbor as yourself.*

She sat with her family, pushed the food around on her plate, stole occasional glances at Zeb. Ada inched closer, lowered her voice and said, "Doesn't really matter if the buggy or the horse is first. Just get over there."

"I don't know what that means, Ada."

"I think you do." Ada kissed her cheek, then hopped up and followed Ethan and baby Peter, who were headed toward the pond.

"She's right." Sarah nodded toward her plate. "You're not eating that food anyway. Might as well do what needs to be done."

How was it that her entire family knew her business? Eunice offered the ham on her plate to the Glicks' dog and scraped the rest of her food into the trash bin. As the couples and families and even old people finished with their meals, they all headed to the pond. So, Eunice went the opposite direction. She did not want to answer any more questions about her mood.

Of course, when she walked around to the back of the barn, she was nearly bowled over by one small boy, straw hat pushed back on his head, a grin adorning his face. "Look at this, Eunice. A rabbit. And it even likes me holding it. Isn't that amazing? I need to show Lydia and Mary."

And then Josh was gone.

Leaving Eunice standing there, alone, and less than five feet from the one person she was trying to avoid.

"Eunice." Zeb's perpetual frown was in place, but he didn't look away. He watched her, as if he was waiting for something. As if he was waiting for her to take the first step toward reconciliation. Which was what he should do, since he'd been in the wrong. She didn't say that though.

She said, "Sorry, I… I didn't mean to interrupt."

"Do you look like you're interrupting? Pretty much just me and the other rabbits back here."

Sure enough, there was a large rabbit hutch with a variety of bunnies. Eunice couldn't resist. She moved closer and peered down. There were tan ones, white ones, brown ones and one fellow that was a combination of all three. She suddenly wanted to pick one up more than she'd wanted anything all day. She opened the gate, stepped inside and reached for the white bunny, which immediately hopped in the other direction.

Zeb cleared his throat as if something were lodged there. "Same thing happened to Josh. He finally cornered one over by the water bowl."

Which worked. She cuddled the tri-colored bunny in the crook of her arm, stepped back through the gate and sat on the bench. What was it about holding a rabbit that made the world feel right? This little guy pushed his nose into the crook of her arm, ears alert, nose twitching back and forth causing her to giggle like a schoolgirl.

"He's not that funny looking."

Zeb had moved closer, and Eunice jumped at the sound of his voice.

"He's tickling my arm." She rearranged the rabbit so that it was looking out and over the bend of her elbow. "That's better."

"Didn't know you were an animal person," Zeb said.

"I live on a farm. Of course I love animals. Plus, I lived with Ada when she first went through her animal rescue phase. Try caring for a blind donkey."

Zeb chuckled. It wasn't a laugh exactly, but it was an improvement over the scowl. "I sense that you're still put out with me."

"Yup."

"And…" He sighed dramatically. "I suppose you have a right to be."

"Yup."

"You're not going to cut me any slack."

"Nope."

"First woman I've met who could answer questions with single syllables."

"So, you've met a lot of women, have you?"

"Not really." He leaned closer, ran a hand down the rabbit's back, sighed again. "I know I've messed up. Just tell me the worst of it and we'll muddle through."

He attempted a smile. It fell flat. Something about that pathetic attempt to lighten the moment ignited the anger that Eunice had been trying to tamp down since Josh fell off the cow.

"Fine. Here." She pushed the rabbit into his arms and began to pace back and first. "Where should I start? You're arrogant."

"Arrogant?"

"You think you're the only one who has ever raised a child. And another thing. You're mopey."

"I'm mopey?"

"All hangdog looks and long sighs. Would it kill you to actually smile at something?"

"I suppose it wouldn't."

Still, she was on a roll. Why stop? "And the thing that gets my goat, the part that makes me want to stomp my foot, is that you're holding my future in your hands."

He'd been petting the rabbit, but now his hands froze. "How so?"

"I've already agreed to be part of your tour, which mind you could be very humiliating to me. I don't know if that was my *dat*'s idea or yours." She held up a hand. "Don't tell me. I don't want to know. My point is that if you up and decide I'm not doing that well—if you fire me again—then it's off to Kentucky for me. Just throw me on a bus and send me away."

She tried to make it sound funny, but that last part came out rather pitiful. Maybe Zeb's solemnness was catching. She turned away from him, rapidly blinking back tears, wishing she were still holding the rabbit.

Eunice heard him stand, walk to the hutch, open the gate and say, "Off with you, little fellow," then close the gate. By the time he'd joined her at the pasture fence, she'd reined in her emotions.

"I'm not arrogant," he said. "I'm afraid."

His words so echoed what Becca had said that Eunice flinched.

"I'm afraid all the time. That I'm going to do something wrong. Something tragically wrong. Something that will cost me not just my wife but also my son."

"Zeb..."

"Let me finish. You've had your say. And I hear your frustration and anger, Eunice. But I have a lot at stake here."

"As do I."

"True. That's true. As for being mopey, yeah, maybe so. Maybe I need...some sort of change."

Something in her heart lurched. "I thought Shipshe was the change you needed?"

"I did too." He walked a few steps down the fence line, stared out past the rabbit enclosure to the trees beyond. "I did too."

Now he turned toward her, all emotion gone, purely business. "But my future is as dependent on you as you claim yours is dependent on me."

"How so?"

"Because if these tours don't work—if my *bruder* and I can't raise the money for a down payment on the farm—then my son loses not just his *mamm* and his grandparents but also the family home. And I'm not going to let that happen, Eunice."

"Okay." Where was he going with this? How was this all her fault?

"We're not children anymore, Eunice. We're adults with adult responsibilities. You were wrong about one thing. It's not my fault if your *dat* sends you to Kentucky. That's on you."

"Me?"

"You're the one that needs to make your agreement with your *dat* work. It's not as if there aren't half a dozen men who would court you in a minute."

"And you could have a new *fraa* anytime—"

"I don't want a new *fraa*." The words sounded as if they'd been torn from his heart.

They stood there, staring at each other.

She'd crossed a line. She shouldn't have gone anywhere near the subject of Suzanne. "I'm sorry."

"*Nein*. Not good enough. You need to help me make this tour work."

"I thought you were doing fine at the market."

"The market's closed, Eunice. If you haven't noticed."

"Oh, yeah. But there's the Christmas market…"

"I can't wait until Christmas."

He stood there, hands on his hips, and again a little of his emotion peeked through. She had a glimpse of his desperation. Was Pennsylvania so bad? Why was he dead set on not moving back there? At least he'd have Suzanne's family to help.

Is that what she wanted?

Did she want Zebedee Mast out of her life for good?

A small voice reminded her that her problems would remain even when he was gone. She realized, in that moment, what she missed was her friend. She missed the guy who understood her and accepted her for who she was. And she wasn't sure that guy even existed anymore. The person standing in front of her? He was no longer that young man who had grown up with her, who had been filled with optimism and fun.

This person—she didn't even know him.

Zeb was still waiting on an answer.

"You certainly don't have to worry about my part of the tour."

"Meaning?"

"Meaning that I'll make sure it's every one of your tourists' favorite stops." And with that pronouncement, she turned and hightailed it back to her family.

She didn't know how she was going to accomplish what she'd just claimed she could and would do. But one way or another, she would see this through. Zeb's life might be miserable. But it wouldn't be miserable because of her.

Chapter Nine

The first few days of the following week flew. Eunice worked at the yarn shop on Monday and Tuesday. Myra Lancaster was determined to teach her how to knit, which wasn't going particularly well.

Eunice could take a small motor apart by touch. She knew where every piece should be, how those parts should feel, what they should do. But give her yarn and two needles, and she was a disaster.

"You're holding it wrong again."

"Oh. Sorry."

"Try to relax."

"Right."

"It's not a fork and knife, you know."

After another grueling fifteen minutes during which she managed to knot up the yarn twice, she was finally released to restock some shelves. At least that was something she could do quickly and correctly. She'd even discovered that she was learning to enjoy the wide variety of colors and the way various types of yarn felt different in her hands. They currently had several autumn displays up, but Myra had ordered quite a bit of reds and greens and golds for Christmas projects which they were going to display the following week.

"We have to start selling it well before Christmas," Myra

explained. "It takes most people several weeks to do a project. By having the holiday colors out the second week of November, we're giving them time to plan."

"Seems as if we're trampling on Thanksgiving."

"Says the woman who's taken a week to knit a pot holder." Myra's words were offered with a smile and a pat on the shoulder.

Eunice laughed. "And still it's the wrong shape—it doesn't even resemble a square. Or a rectangle for that matter. It's more like a trapezoid."

"Don't give up, my dear. Some things simply require perseverance."

Eunice thought about that as she drove away. Maybe Zeb required perseverance. Why was it that he was stuck in her head? He wasn't her problem. Not really. So why did she feel responsible for him?

Like she did at least once an hour, she forced her thoughts in another direction. She needed some small engine projects for tomorrow's first tour. Local farmers had stopped bringing her their broken things. They'd figured—rightly—that she didn't have time to work on them.

But now working on broken things would once again be her job. At least for three days a week. The thought brought a smile to her face. She stopped off at the Gold farm. Saul Gold had worked his eighty-acre place all of his life, or at least all of Eunice's life. He had an old generator that had stopped working.

"Comes in handy during birthing season," he said. "We hook up a few lights to help us attend to the cows. Maybe some heaters if they're needed." He cackled revealing a missing front tooth. "Even have me one of those *Englisch* coffeepots, but I only use it during the birthing nights when we need coffee at the ready—strong and hot."

Eunice assured him she could fix the generator, thanked him and together they loaded the contraption into her buggy.

Her next stop was at Ethan's, who had a solar pump he'd tried in vain to fix himself. "I might have made it worse," he admitted.

"No worries. I'll have this up and running by the weekend."

She popped her head into the house on Huckleberry Lane long enough to say hello to Ada and baby Peter, then set off for home.

Two hours later, she heard the rattle of buggy wheels and realized *Dat* was home. She hadn't even started dinner!

"Don't worry about it," he said, surveying all that she'd set up in the barn. "This looks *gut*. I think the tourists will enjoy hearing what you have to say."

"And if the weather holds—"

"It's supposed to, according to the Shipshe forecast."

"Then we'll be golden." She wiped her hands on a rag. "Want me to run in and rustle up something for us to eat?"

"I can put together sandwiches and a small salad. You finish up here."

As Eunice made her way back into the barn, she felt something like hope blossom in her chest. She was good at this. She knew what parts went where, how to correct things, how to put them back together again. And she loved the way the barn smelled. The way every tool was in the specially designated place that she had created for it.

More importantly than those things was her *dat*'s attitude. As she walked toward the house, jogged up the stairs and into the kitchen, she realized that he did want her to succeed. He wanted her to have a full and healthy life. The issue was that they differed on what that included. For her *dat*, it meant a home, marriage and children. Eunice didn't know if she wanted those things. She'd decided at a pretty young age that given her interests and talents, marriage might not happen for her.

Maybe insisting that she be financially independent was a good compromise. It was something she could work toward.

She slept well that night.

The next day, she wasn't nervous at all. Okay, maybe a little, but not nearly as nervous as she was when Myra put a pair of knitting needles in her hands. Those things were sharp.

The first tour group was due to arrive at two thirty in the afternoon. She'd seen Zeb's buggy when he'd dropped Josh off at Becca's. She was a little surprised that Josh hadn't jogged over to see her, but perhaps that was forbidden. Whatever. She didn't need Zeb's approval. She only needed the tour to be successful.

The day's tourists included four couples and a group of women that numbered six. That made for fourteen guests. Eunice had borrowed folding chairs from the market and set them up in a semicircle facing her workbench.

"Welcome," she said, once everyone was settled.

They responded with a hearty "Hello" and "Howdy" and a few waves. Eunice noticed the men scanning the barn. She imagined they were comparing what they were seeing here with what they saw back home, or—if they lived in a city now—what they were familiar with from their childhood.

"I hope you have enjoyed your tour so far."

There was much nodding and murmuring and some thumbs-ups.

"That Naomi Schwartz is something. How she manages to sew with so many little ones is beyond me."

"And with a treadle machine," one of the older women added.

"*Ya*. True. Our community doesn't have electricity in our

homes, as you probably know. The treadle machine allows Naomi to sew more quickly than if she did so by hand, but still she is within the parameters of our church. So, it might surprise you to see that I'm working on a few gadgets here that appear somewhat untraditional for Amish folk." She lowered her voice, getting into the rhythm of her speech and responding to the smiles from the group. "My bishop even knows about it, so there's no need to keep it on the down-low."

More laughter, but now they were sitting up straight, looking interested.

"We Amish treasure the old ways. Naomi's sewing. Martha's quilting. And, of course, the way that Jess farms. These are time-honored traditions that we pass down from generation to generation."

Zeb entered the back of the barn and took a spot to the side—standing with his arms crossed. Watching. Listening. Evaluating. She forced her attention away from him and back to the group of folks hanging on her every word.

"Even our clothes, as you can see, are old-fashioned. Not so very different from the clothes my *mamm* and *grossmammi* wore as young women." She folded her hands together and waited, knowing they were now inspecting her. They were seeing her. "My clothes are a little different though. When my *grossmammi* was a young woman, Amish women wore mostly gray or black dresses covered with a white apron."

"Your dress is a pretty pastel blue."

"Danki." Eunice smiled at the *Englisch* woman with short red hair. "Each Amish community makes rules for what is acceptable. That's called our *Ordnung.* Those are local decisions. They're not something that's passed down from any centralized church."

Several of the group nodded.

"My community has, over the years, decided that pastel

colors are fine. Our goal is to not draw attention to ourselves. We strive to remain humble, to remain Plain. But we like a little color in our wardrobe as much as the next gal."

Robust laughter.

"In the same way, we are allowed a bit of latitude in the jobs we choose. Now, you probably won't be seeing an Amish person working the window of a Starbucks drive-through, but my youngest *schweschder*, Ada, works for the local SPCA. Becca, another *schweschder*, has gone on several mission trips with Mennonite Disaster Services."

"They came to Texas a few times," an older man offered. "Amazing what those folks did. This was after the last hurricane came through. The MDS people built houses for everyone who needed one."

"Becca would be happy to talk with you about her experience working on mission trips," Eunice said. "You'll be stopping by her house for some refreshments in a few minutes. It's a three-minute walk that way."

She jerked her thumb in the direction of Becca's house and everyone smiled.

"Today what I wanted to talk to you about is the way we incorporate some forms of technology into our lives, and how much I enjoy working on small engines."

Eunice limited her talk to fifteen minutes, then opened it up to Q&A. Fortunately, there were plenty of questions, and they were deep into a discussion of the benefits and challenges of solar energy when she looked up and saw Becca standing next to Zeb. Baby Abram was on her hip. Mary stood next to Joshua.

"And now, I believe my *schweschder* would like to offer you some refreshments."

As the group filed out of the barn, thanking her and saying

what a wonderful time they had, Joshua ran to the front and threw his arms around her legs, nearly knocking her over.

"Eunice. I haven't seen you in, like, forever."

"You saw her Sunday, son." Zeb had followed Josh to where Eunice was seeing everyone out, though he didn't greet her with the same exuberance as his son. In fact, he looked... well, she couldn't quite name the expression on his face.

Puzzled?

Confused?

Disoriented?

Little Mary tapped Josh on the arm and said, "You're it." Which was all it took for the two of them to dash out into the afternoon's waning sunlight.

"Well?" Eunice asked. "How was it?"

"*Ya.* You did well. You're apparently a natural at this."

"Hmm. If you're pleased, you should tell your face."

Instead of being offended, Zeb shrugged and offered the smallest of smiles. "I've heard that I'm arrogant and gloomy."

"Mopey. I said you were mopey." Refusing to let his attitude ruin her good mood, Eunice smiled. "Think I'll go enjoy some of Becca's refreshments."

"*Ya.* Good idea." He fell in step with her.

"This group seems like an easy-to-please lot."

"They are." He nodded. "But I believe you caught them by surprise."

"Oh?"

"From what I've heard in the few tours I've already done, a lot of these women—even some of the men—read Amish fiction."

"Oh?"

"So they were probably expecting the sewing and quilting and farming."

"Right."

"But a modern Amish woman? Now that's one they'll be telling their friends about back home."

"Which is a good thing. Right?"

"Sure. Word of mouth sells tickets."

"And tickets plus tips help to pay the bills."

"And the farm down payment."

"Right." Eunice stopped on the top step. "How's that going, by the way?"

"Pretty good, actually. I met with a loan officer, and they're considering our application."

"That's *gut*, right?"

"It is."

If his application was accepted, they would stay.

Why did that feel very important to her? Eunice could hear Becca talking to the guests, offering lemonade, coffee, hot tea. The smell of freshly baked cookies wafted out toward them. She closed her eyes, felt the warmth of the sun and the satisfaction of a day that had gone well.

Then she opened her eyes and saw Zeb studying her. "Think I'll help myself to a few cookies."

"Ya?" He raised one eyebrow. The right one. She suddenly remembered how he'd done that in school when he'd been surprised by something. The little boy she'd grown up with was still in there somewhere, just fighting to get out.

"Come on. I can even score you a hot or cold beverage— your pick."

"Sounds like you have an *in* with the cook."

"Indeed, I do, my friend. Indeed, I do."

Eunice knew her problems weren't solved. Her *dat* still wanted to push her out of the proverbial nest, and here she was contentedly dropping back into it. It didn't feel the same though. She felt different from the young woman who had been issued an ultimatum only two months before.

And part of her was even excited about how these changes in her life were going to turn out.

Zeb understood that he should have been happy. All three tours that week had gone well. Tips were better than he'd expected, which had made all involved optimistic about the venture. Everyone seemed to think that they were off to a strong start. Even Amos commented on the results he'd had from the online survey form.

But Zeb wasn't happy.

He was prickly. That was the best word for it. Suzanne used to call him that when he was fussy because there hadn't been enough rain for the newly planted crops. Or because there'd been too much rain. "I don't control the weather, dear. Talk to *Gotte* if you want to lodge a complaint." Then she'd pointed to the ceiling, toward heaven, and smiled.

Suzanne hadn't tolerated his moodiness.

Now that she wasn't around, he felt himself falling back into that low place. And this time it was lower than ever. Of course, it was. He was a widower. Two years and he still wasn't used to the reality of that statement.

He and Samuel had made it a habit to walk down to the phone booth and call their parents on Saturday afternoons. Samuel had spoken first, for about ten minutes, then handed the phone to Josh.

"I'm off, *bruder*," he said in a low voice. "Don't wait up for me."

Zeb didn't ask where he was going or how late he'd be home. Samuel still enjoyed hanging out with a group of friends, and there was more than one young lady that he'd been dating. He was pulling his weight as far as contributing to the finances, so there was no reason for Zeb to criticize him. Plus, he was the younger brother.

Josh was on the phone next, describing his stays at Becca's to his *grossmammi*. Zeb decided to save her from the protracted point-by-point description of what they did, what they ate and how often they played tag.

"Tell your *grossmammi* you love her and hand me the phone."

Josh did, with great enthusiasm.

Zeb covered the mouthpiece and reminded him to "Stay close."

"Got it, *Dat*. Don't get dirty. Don't get hurt. I got it." He preceded to walk over to a tree and attempt to climb it.

Zeb spoke to his *mamm*, trying to keep it light, trying to keep the worry out of his voice, but there was no hiding things from her. She knew him too well.

"I can tell you're not feeling any better."

"Nothing's changed. Why should I feel better?"

"Maybe you should see a doctor." His *mamm*'s tone was patient but firm.

"I'm not sick."

"Depression is a kind of sickness, Zeb."

"I don't know that I'm depressed. I'm grieving. That's different."

"Maybe it is and maybe it isn't. The thing is that you seem stuck."

He couldn't argue with that.

"And stuck isn't where you want to be, especially when you're raising a five-year-old boy."

Ah, more guilt. That was exactly what he needed.

"Have you talked with Ezekiel? He's a *gut* man and a *wunderbaar* bishop. He will give you solid advice."

How did they get on the topic of his moods? Zeb changed the subject to her arthritis—which was better. His father—who was down at the rec center playing shuffleboard. Even the weather—sunny and cool, but not cold. No snow in the forecast.

When he ran out of things to ask her about, she switched the subject right back to him. "What about dating? Have you given that any more thought?"

"I need to go, *Mamm*."

"Promise me you'll think about what we've said."

"Sure, *ya*. Of course." And he wasn't lying. He had no doubts her words—her suggestions—would go round and round in his head as he tried to go to sleep that night.

"We love you and Josh and Samuel very much."

"We love you too."

He hung up, trying to push her words from his mind.

Where was his son? Why couldn't he stay where he was supposed to just this one time? Then he heard a giggle from above.

"Come down, son. And don't tear your clothes on those branches."

Josh hopped down in front of him. "I'm *gut* at tree climbing and tree jumping. See?"

Dirty, but nothing seemed torn…or broken.

"Let's walk back."

"It was nice talking to *Mammi*, right?"

"Loved every minute of it."

Josh had picked up a small tree branch which he was whacking against each fence post they passed. "You don't seem happy, *Dat*. Is it because of me?"

Zeb stopped in his tracks. He stopped so suddenly that Josh kept walking, realized he was alone, then turned back and cocked his head. "Am I in trouble?"

"Nein."

"Great. That's a relief."

"Josh, come here a minute." He knelt down on the dirt

road so that he'd be eye to eye with his son. "When I'm in a bad mood, it's not because of you."

"Except when I'm really dirty."

"Okay, maybe then."

"Or I spill something like milk, which is super hard to clean up."

"Right, but my point is that I love you, and yes, I'm a little blue sometimes, but it's just something I have to work through."

"Okay." Josh was now using his stick to make zigzag marks in the dirt. Finally, he looked up. "Is it because of *Mamm*? Because she's gone?"

How was he supposed to answer that? "I miss her," he finally admitted.

"Me too."

A small wind shook leaves from a nearby tree and sent them sailing to the ground. Josh leaped toward them with his stick, striking out and missing them. It occurred to Zeb in that moment that Josh was ready to move forward, but he couldn't. His son couldn't move past Suzanne's death because Zeb was holding him back.

That night after putting Josh to bed, instead of scrubbing the kitchen clean, he decided it was time to do something about the state of his soul, of his heart. He probably should read his Bible more often. No doubt, the answers to his many questions were within its pages. He had to search again for the book which he thought he'd left beside the bed, but the small table was covered with a pile of clean clothes.

When he did find it, the Bible had a thin layer of dust across the top. He used the cuff of his sleeve to wipe the cover clean, and he remembered that it had been a gift from his parents when he'd finished his schooling at the end of eighth grade. The fact that he'd allowed it to become buried under a pile of laundry was a terrible indication that he wasn't really looking for answers. At least, he wasn't looking for them in the one place that he knew held answers.

Pouring himself a cup of decaf, he grabbed two of the cookies Becca had sent home and went to the front porch. The temperature was turning colder, so he wore his jacket.

The sun had already set, Josh was asleep and the evening was lovely. He could do this. He could open the pages of his Bible and read. Maybe the solution to his heartache was there. Surely, it was. But he hadn't even brought a lantern or flashlight.

He didn't have the energy to go back inside, so he sat there in the dark. Sipping the coffee. Eating the cookie though he didn't taste it. He couldn't have said if it was oatmeal or chocolate chip. His hand rested on the Bible, and he closed his eyes. He tried to pray. What was he supposed to say? Where did he even begin? His mind went blank—totally, completely blank. And then he began to hear the words of his *mamm.*

Maybe you should see a doctor.

Depression is a kind of sickness.

Have you talked with Ezekiel?

He could do that. He could speak with the bishop. Ezekiel would direct him. Ezekiel would pray with him, guide him through the scripture, help him find a doctor. The next day was an off-Sunday, and they had been invited to Ezekiel's for dinner.

Zeb had considered coming up with an excuse and not attending. But that would be a cowardly thing to do. He owed his son more than that. Josh loved seeing other children his age, playing after the meal, spending time outside. Zeb couldn't cancel because he was a coward.

You don't seem happy, Dat. *Is it because of me?*

He was a failure as a father. It was actually embarrassing

how badly he was coping. But he didn't have to stay in the terrible place that he'd fallen into. He could find a way out. He could do it for Joshua.

He would go to the luncheon, and he'd speak to the bishop.

An image of Eunice popped into his mind, but he pushed it away. She'd been right that he was arrogant and mopey, but he couldn't think about Eunice right now. He needed to think about Joshua.

It was time for something to change.

It was time to do whatever he needed to do to get unstuck.

Chapter Ten

❧

Eunice was back at the yarn shop Monday morning. She enjoyed Mondays because the business was technically closed. She didn't have to interact with customers who had perfectly legitimate questions about yarn and stitches, crocheting and knitting, tension and whether or not to block their work. Eunice couldn't answer any of those questions. She figured she could fill a book with the things she didn't know. Which didn't bother her as much as it had at first. She would learn. Myra was determined to teach her. As for this fine Monday, she was able to spend the entire day stocking shelves, updating the window displays and pricing items.

She was surprised when Myra used her key to unlock the front door and walked in with a tall dark-haired man who looked to be in his late twenties or early thirties. His clothes were conservative—dark pants and a blue cotton button-up shirt. He didn't have a phone glued to the palm of his hand like many of their customers. She didn't think he was Amish, but he wasn't *Englisch*, but he wasn't *Englisch*, which probably meant he was Mennonite.

"Eunice. I'm so glad you're here. I just shared a coffee with my cousin, Lester. He's from over in Goshen."

"Good to meet you." He didn't offer his hand to shake, but

he walked closer and beamed at her. "Myra tells me you're learning to knit."

"I hope she wasn't giving you horror stories about my mistakes over coffee."

"Ha. Nope. She actually said you're a good employee and a valuable part of her retail team." He lowered his voice in a mock whisper. "She speaks like she's *Englisch* sometimes."

Myra shook her head in amusement. "There's nothing wrong with being business savvy. And before you make fun of that, I'm going to go find the retailer information I promised you. Give me a second."

Uh-oh. Was she supposed to entertain Lester until Myra returned? She needn't have worried. He walked around the shop, picking up things and setting them back down.

"Looking for anything in particular?"

"Nope. I don't knit." He smiled again. "My sisters do though. This would be a great place to buy them a gift."

"Believe me we have all types of yarn and doodads, which is not the official name for knitting accessories and supplies."

Lester perched on a stool she'd pulled out of the storeroom. Sometimes it was nice to sit while she was restocking, and Eunice usually drug it around the store with her on Mondays.

"What retailer information is Myra fetching? Surely you don't need to purchase that much yarn for your *schweschdern*."

"Nope. I am not interested in purchasing yarn in bulk. My *aenti* is opening a craft shop in Goshen, and she doesn't know who to purchase display racks from."

"Ah. We definitely have plenty of those." Eunice resumed hanging packets of stitch stoppers on a rotating display. This new order they'd received featured cute little farm animals. They were made of rubber and used to put on the end of needles while you were in the middle of a project so the stitches didn't fall off. Hence the name *stitch stoppers*. She almost explained all of that to Lester, then realized he would not care about stitch stoppers.

"Myra tells me you're a real whiz with electronics."

"Not electronics as much as small engines."

"And you know how to fix them?"

"I do. I'm the proverbial black sheep—an Amish woman who doesn't knit or quilt or sew. Plus, I often have grease under my fingertips." She inspected her fingertips, sure she'd managed to banish any residue of grease, but nope…right pointer finger had a thin line of black under the nail. She held it up and shrugged.

Lester laughed, which served to put Eunice at ease. He hadn't been offended or shocked by her revelation. He hadn't even looked at her like she was a bizarre creature simply because she enjoyed working on small engines. And he didn't ply her with a thousand questions. Instead, they moved on to talking about fall festivals and Thanksgiving plans. He worked at the Mennonite college in Goshen. "I'm not a full professor, not yet. Just finished my undergraduate work and this semester I'm starting on my master's degree."

"What field?"

"Literature. I'm something of a bookworm," he confessed.

Myra bustled back into the room, and Eunice returned to her work. Lester made a point to say goodbye to her before he left.

"It was nice to meet you," he said.

"*Ya.* You too."

She didn't give the encounter much thought, but the next morning he called up to ask if they had stitch markers.

"I have no idea what those are," he admitted. "But my

schweschder said she'd love to have some for Christmas—
a not too subtle hint."

"Actually, I just put more out on the display racks. We
have all kinds. I'm sure Myra would be happy to set some
back for you." She thought the conversation would end there,
but they ended up talking about books. When he asked her,
she shared that her favorite book was *Little Women*. "I could
always relate to Jo," she confessed.

"So you were something of a tomboy?"

"Still am, actually. I've stopped climbing trees, but I still
enjoy working in the barn." It was mid-morning, and there
was no one in the shop. She was manning the register, but
since there was no one to check out she leaned on the counter
and enjoyed the conversation with a charming man whom
she'd just met.

He told her about some of his students and how much he
was looking forward to the holiday break. She told him about
the tours, how much she'd enjoyed the first three, how much
she was looking forward to the next one.

"I have one more class to teach, but if it's okay, I'll stop
by and pick up some of those stitch markers around three."

"Sure. I leave at two thirty, but I'll put your name on the
items."

"Not necessary. I can rearrange my afternoon meetings.
I'll be there by two."

The rest of the morning flew, lunchtime was busy and
then things settled down. When the bell over the door rang at
two o'clock on the dot she nearly fell off her stool. This time,
Lester was wearing a white cotton shirt and black pants.

"You're back."

"I am."

They spoke for a good fifteen minutes. Lester seemed interested in whatever she had to say. Eunice wasn't used to that

sort of attention, especially from a man. She found herself comparing him to Zeb. Lester was probably an inch taller. Both were thin, but Lester didn't have the same muscular look about him that Zeb had. Since Lester made his living teaching literature, that made sense to her.

Eunice thought it was funny that he'd missed seeing Myra, who had stepped out for a quick errand. "She should be back soon."

"Oh, that's okay. I like talking to you."

Eunice blushed, unsure how to answer that.

"Say, would you like to go out this weekend?"

"Go out?"

"Yeah. Surely, you've heard of the custom. I pick you up, we go somewhere, maybe enjoy a meal."

She laughed. "I know what *going out* means. I was just surprised, is all."

"Why would you be surprised?"

"Because you're a college graduate and I spend my time working on small engines or stocking shelves in a yarn shop."

"Both are perfectly respectable jobs."

"I guess you're right. They are."

"So, is that a yes?"

Her mind flashed to Zeb, then Josh. She pushed the images away. Zeb had made it quite clear that he was not interested in being anything more than her friend, and at times she wasn't even sure about that.

"It's a yes. I'd love to." She pulled a piece of paper off the notepad by the register and wrote her address on it.

"Four o'clock Friday?"

"Better make it five. I have a tour."

"Right." His eyes danced. "Tours—your other job. I can't wait to hear more about it."

She walked around the rest of the day in a bit of a daze.

She couldn't believe it. She, Eunice Yoder, had a date. It was a little frightening to think about that, but hadn't she vowed to start taking steps forward in her life? She had. And this was a nice solid step. She. Had. A. Date.

And she hadn't even needed her *dat* to set it up.

Imagine that.

Zeb had thought the day was going well. It wasn't that he felt immediately better after his revelation over the weekend, but he had the sense that he was at least moving in the right direction. Then, Eunice had mentioned that she was going on a date with some guy named Lester whom she'd met in the yarn shop and was Mennonite. He wasn't even Amish!

"You can't go out with a Mennonite."

"Excuse me?" The look she gave him dared him to *go there*.

"What I mean is—" Zeb's words stumbled, then ground to a halt.

"Go on. This should be interesting."

They were standing at the back of Becca's kitchen. The weather had turned cold and blustery, and he thought they might have snow before the weekend was over. Which was fine with him. He didn't mind a little snow. Covered everything up real nice and made it all look pretty and clean. Made for a nice buggy ride too.

No doubt, Lester drove a car not a buggy. He thought about pointing that out to Eunice, but she might think that was a plus instead of a negative. She might like riding in *Englisch* automobiles.

"What does your *dat* say?"

"What does my *dat* say?" Eunice was looking at him with her eyebrows arched high and the expression on her face indicating that the top of her head might blow off. "Zeb, that's

none of your business. But since you're interested, he said—
and this is a direct quote—'I hope you have a good time.'"

He would have left it at that, would have left her there in
the kitchen, but the sitting room was full of *Englischers*, and
it was cold outside.

They stood there in awkward silence for a moment. When
had things become so awkward between them? He'd always
felt more comfortable around Eunice than anyone else in
school. When had that changed?

Adulthood was not all it was cracked up to be.

She sighed heavily and stared down into her coffee mug.
He could hear Josh and Mary playing in the next room. Becca
was describing one of her mission trips to the guests. Zeb
folded his arms and scowled at the opposite wall.

Eunice rinsed out her mug and set it in the sink. She was
about to leave the room when Zeb sank into a chair at the table
and said, "I spoke with Ezekiel on Monday."

"Oh?"

He pushed out the adjacent chair with his foot. He was
hoping she'd take that small gesture as an invitation and sit
down. She did, and then he wasn't sure what to say.

"Do you want to talk about it?"

"I don't know."

"Okay."

They sat there, silent for another moment, and then Zeb
admitted, "Earlier today I saw a doctor in Goshen."

He looked at Eunice and his heart skipped a beat. He knew
that wasn't really a thing. Suzanne had sometimes read romance books tagged with Inspirational Romance—which
was supposed to mean they were faith based. She would
check them out from the library and then read him parts.
She loved finding the lines where someone's heart skipped
a beat, and then she'd get the giggles.

But looking at Eunice, who was waiting for him to explain this conversation he had started—a conversation he wasn't certain he was ready to have—it really did feel like his heart hesitated, then decided to continue beating.

"Are you okay?" Eunice asked.

"*Nein.* Apparently, I'm clinically depressed."

"Oh. I could have saved you the money and told you that." She didn't seem to mean it flippantly.

The way she was looking at him, he thought that she was actually feeling compassion for him, for his situation. So instead of arguing with her, he simply nodded.

"It's been two years since Suzanne's passing. Right?"

"Yup. That's one of the differences between grief and depression. Grief is a normal thing people go through." He glanced up and searched for understanding in her eyes. Finally, he said, "Like your family did when your *mamm* passed."

"*Ya.* That's true. I can remember a heavy cloud that hung over my family during that time. I was quite young—only four—but a four-year-old still notices things. Even a child can tell when the people around them are sad."

He thought of Josh. Thought of the way his son had looked at him when he'd asked if Zeb's sadness was because of him. He closed his eyes and heard the boy's laughter coming from the next room.

"Grief is normal, but what I'm going through isn't. It's depression." He attempted to chuckle, but it fell flat.

"Don't be embarrassed."

"Because I can't handle a natural part of life? Why would that embarrass me?" He sat back in the chair, crossed his arms and stared at the doorway that led from the kitchen to the sitting room. "Apparently, I've allowed myself to become isolated. Honestly, I would skip church if I could get away with it. But the last thing I want is more people wondering what's wrong with me."

"Why do you think that is? Why would you rather be alone?" Eunice waited, looking quite interested in his answer.

Had she been able to sense that he didn't want to be there when they had church services or luncheons? Had everyone noticed? He'd thought he'd done such a good job of hiding what he was feeling, but perhaps that wasn't true. Perhaps his pain had been obvious to everyone but him. Because he'd refused to look at it. He'd refused to deal with it.

"I guess because I think no one understands what I'm going through."

"Some do."

"Yup. That's what Doctor Ellington said." He shrugged, met her gaze for a second before he resumed staring at the doorway. "Seeking isolation, feeling disconnected and shunning support. Those are the three big things that distinguish depression from grief." He peeked back at her and almost laughed.

Eunice looked as if she wanted to jump up and shout *glory, hallelujah.*

"This is a positive turn of events," she said.

"It is?"

"Yes. Since you've been back, you've reminded me of a tomcat that wants to come inside, but also doesn't want to let anyone near."

"You're comparing me to a tomcat?"

She shrugged, and he couldn't help smiling. He could trust Eunice to tell him what she was really thinking. She wasn't one to hold on to something then say it behind your back. It was one of many things he liked about her.

"That took courage, Zeb. Going to Bishop Ezekiel—well, we all do that at one time or another."

"You have?"

"Of course. I was so upset when my *dat* first came up with the Kentucky ultimatum that I went to speak with him several times. He helped me to see that my *dat* loves me and is trying to help me through a difficult time. The problem was that I didn't see my situation as difficult. I saw it as the perfect life." She drummed her fingers against the table. "But going to see a doctor, that must have been hard. Amish barely go when they're physically sick. It's even more rare for us to go for mental health."

"Funny that you use that phrase—mental health. It's not one we toss around every often."

"Both Ethan and Aaron struggled with family issues. And their *dat*, well, he was in the hospital in Goshen more than once to help treat his bipolar disorder."

He again looked directly at her. "I didn't know that."

"Yup. Then their parents moved—"

"Like mine."

"But for different reasons. Esther didn't know what else to do. This was after the fire that Zachary had unintentionally caused. She insisted they move to Florida to be near her parents. Esther insisted that she needed help."

"Wow."

"Yup."

Guests began filing into the kitchen, putting their dishes in the sink, thanking Eunice and Zeb and Becca. They all hurried back to their tour vehicle, which was Jocelyn's van. She'd gone outside to turn it on a few minutes earlier, so it would be nice and toasty when the tourists climbed back in. Many of the tourists waved from behind the windows as Jocelyn drove away.

Eunice and Zeb and Becca stood on the porch, coats pulled tight, watching the van drive down the lane. Zeb didn't go back into town with them, since his place was on this side of Shipshe, like the Yoders'. It was all working out quite well, which was something that surprised him.

"I feel like we're doing important work here," Becca said.

"How so?" Zeb kind of agreed with her, but he didn't know how to put it into words. He was interested in her answer. How could a little farm tour be important?

"Think of it this way. We're helping people step away from the stress and loneliness of their lives. You don't have to be Plain to know your neighbor or to help one another. You don't have to be Amish to share tea and cookies with a neighbor."

"We don't have all the answers," Eunice pointed out.

"Indeed, we don't." Becca grinned broadly, then walked back into the house leaving Zeb and Eunice to watch the season's first snowflakes fall.

Josh and Mary dashed out past them and into the lightly swirling snow. Laughing. Twirling in circles. Holding their heads back and trying to catch a snowflake on their tongues. Talking about the first snowmen of the season. It reminded Zeb of when he and Eunice were young. When they used to run and play at recess and lunch. It seemed that Eunice had always been a part of his life, as she was now.

He had a sudden urge to reach for her hand. He didn't. It would probably scare her to death. She was a *gut* friend, and he needed to tell her that he appreciated her.

Not today though. He'd do it another time. He'd do it when they had a few moments alone.

Chapter Eleven

Zeb tried not to think about Eunice going out on a date. She had her *dat*'s permission, not that she technically needed it. Still, Amos had apparently told her to have a good time, so who was he to think it was a terrible idea?

The guy was Mennonite.

He was apparently older, at least by a few years.

And she barely knew him.

Three good reasons that she should have said no.

He explained as much to his *bruder*, Samuel, as they did the dinner dishes. His counselor had suggested he try to restore his relationship with his family. That was the word he'd used. *Restore*. As if they were two nations creating an alliance or negotiating a treaty.

"You're just jealous," Samuel said.

"What?" The word came out more emphatic than he'd intended. *The lady doth protest too much.* Only he wasn't a lady. He was an Amish farmer. "I am not."

"Didn't your doctor say for you to start being honest with yourself? You have feelings for Eunice. Anyone with eyes can see it."

Now Zeb groaned. But instead of stomping out of the room, he took a deep breath and set to scouring the pan that he'd burned the bacon in. He was not the best cook. Some days, breakfast for dinner was the best he could do and still he'd burned it. *Focus on the positive.* That was another saying of his counselor's. Okay. He could do that. They'd had a nice meal together.

"Tell me why you think that. Because I'm going to be honest, I haven't consciously thought of Eunice in that way." He'd thought of holding her hand, but that was different. Wasn't it?

"Doesn't surprise me. It's not as if you're in touch with your feelings."

"Says the guy who is dating three women."

"But all three women know that I'm not ready to be in a serious relationship. And they know about each other. We're more friends than we are romantically involved."

Huh. He hadn't thought of it that way.

"But we were talking about your feelings for Eunice."

"I don't know. She's been my friend for a long time."

"She's practically the only person you talk to—besides family."

That was true. But did he think of her as more than a friend? It was hard to even begin to untangle his feelings for her. He supposed it was true that she was his best friend. Maybe, at this point, his only friend.

"Do you find yourself thinking about her when she's not around?"

"Sometimes." How often did he think about Eunice? "I mean pretty often, but then we work together—with the tours and all."

Samuel let that sit between them a few minutes. Finally, he continued as if Zeb hadn't spoken. "And you're jealous about this date she's going on."

"I'm not jealous. I just think it's a bad idea."

Samuel stopped drying dishes and leaned with his back

against the counter. "How would you feel if Hannah Glick were dating a Mennonite guy?"

"Hannah Glick?"

"You know Hannah." Samuel began twirling the dish towel. "You've known her as long as you've known Eunice."

"But I don't know her well."

"True. Let's look at it this way. How would you characterize your relationship with Eunice? Friend? Family? Or something more?"

"That sounds like a quiz in an *Englisch* magazine."

"You got me. I read them sometimes while I'm waiting between auctions. People leave them lying around, so why not educate myself?"

"On how you feel about a girl?" Zeb started to laugh. His brother had always seemed so confident, so sure of everything. He couldn't imagine him ticking answers off on an *Englisch* love quiz.

"Back to the question," Samuel said, a smile tugging at his lips. "Friend? Family? Or something more?"

"Not family. Not really."

"Okay."

"She is my friend, but..."

"But so is Hannah and you wouldn't care who she dates."

Zeb shook his head and turned back to the sink. He let the dish water out, cleaned the sink, rinsed the dishrag and set it across the partition between the wash side and the rinse side. "Okay. I'll be honest enough to say you stumped me. If I have thought of Eunice in that way, in a romantic way, I wasn't aware of it."

"Well, now that you're getting in touch with your feelings, maybe you can figure it out."

At that point, Josh streaked through the kitchen wearing only a bath towel. Zeb was actually relieved to be interrupted.

Samuel left to meet one of his friends, and Zeb spent the next hour with his son. They stored the bath toys. Straightened his bedroom. Played a game of cards—Go Fish, which had been Josh's favorite game for the last few months. Finally, they shared a before-bedtime snack of milk and freshly baked cookies.

"Becca's a *gut* cook."

"That she is," Zeb agreed. He remembered sitting on the porch, just a few nights earlier, unable to taste the cookies he was eating. Those cookies had also been from Becca, so it wasn't that one batch was from a *gut* cook and one from a bad. Nope. He was the one who had changed.

The cookies were peanut butter. They were sweet and crispy. Just like Suzanne made. He let that thought wash over him, closed his eyes, focused on breathing in and out.

"What?" Josh asked.

Zeb opened his eyes. Josh looked worried. He even put his cookie back on the plate—half-eaten. Zeb was learning that his son missed very little. The counselor had suggested he start being more honest with his son.

"I was just thinking about your *mamm*."

"You were?"

"She was a *gut* cook too."

"I don't remember that." Josh frowned, then picked up his cookie and took another bite. Staring at the portion that was left in his hand, he cocked his head, then said, "I'll bet you miss that."

"Yup. I do."

Josh finished the cookie, wiped his fingertips on a napkin, then set the napkin down next to the glass that still held a couple inches of milk. He did each thing very carefully, as if he were trying not to knock something over. Trying not to mess this up. His five-year-old son stood in front of Zeb, who was sitting on the couch. Putting both of his small hands on Zeb's shoulders, he said, "Becca tells us to hug it out."

"Who is *us*?"

"Me and Mary. When we fuss over something."

"You and Mary fuss?"

"It's no big deal, *Dat*. People disagree. Or sometimes one person is sad because they had a terrible breakfast or broke their favorite toy. Anyway, Becca says when you hug it out, everything is better." And then Josh leaned forward, attempted to circle his arms around Zeb's shoulders and squeezed, even giving it an "mmm-hmm" before letting go.

Stepping back, he asked, "Better?"

"Actually, yes."

"Wanna play one more game of cards?"

"Okay, but just one."

"Don't get sad if you lose again."

"You think you can beat me twice?"

Josh's answer was laughter as he began counting out cards for each of them. That sound, that laughter, was enough to make Zeb's day one that he would put in the plus column. Maybe the first such day in a very long time. After Josh was tucked into bed, he sat out on the porch. Allowed himself to simply rock. Listened to the night sounds. Relaxed.

And wondered if there was any chance Samuel was right about Eunice. He didn't think so, but then what did he know? He'd become a master of misdirection—even to himself. Did he care for Eunice in a romantic way? And if he did, was he willing to follow those feelings and see where they led?

Eunice went on the date with Lester Friday evening, so of course when she returned from working at the knit shop on Saturday afternoon, her oldest *schweschder*, Sarah, was in the kitchen.

"I wasn't expecting to see you today," Eunice said, dropping down into one of the kitchen chairs.

"Oh, I just had a few casseroles to bring over and pop in the freezer."

"*Dat* and I are getting by okay, you know."

"Of course you are." Sarah sat down across from her and pushed a bowl of snack mix toward her. "I tried adding raisins, cranberries and chocolate chips in this one."

"*Englischers* sell this in bags."

"But mine is better."

Eunice took a handful, tried it and nodded in agreement. "Yours is better."

"Becca's going to sell them." Sarah beamed as she sat back. "The whole family is getting involved in this tour thing."

"That's how I still think of it too. 'The tour thing.'"

They both laughed.

"So, that's it? You didn't come to quiz me about my date?"

"I did not." Sarah grinned and waited. When Eunice didn't jump in, she added, "But feel free to spill all the details."

"Actually, there's not that much to tell."

"Hmm."

"What?"

"Well, it was your first date in a while. Right?"

"Over a year, actually." Eunice picked up a copy of the *Budget* to fan herself. "That's rather embarrassing to admit."

"Okay. First date in over a year and you have nothing to say about it?"

Eunice reached for another handful of trail mix. "I guess it was okay. Nothing great. I found myself wondering what all the fuss was about."

"Hmm."

"You said that already."

"Maybe I'm saying it because you keep stumping me."

Sarah craned her neck to the left, then the right. "Was he polite?"

"*Ya.* Very."

"Interesting?"

"In his way, I suppose so. He's an English professor, so his world is pretty different from mine."

"Was he attentive?"

"What do you mean?"

"Did he ask about your work or your hobbies? Anything like that?"

"Oh, *ya.* He wanted to hear about the tours and my work on small engines. We shared a few laughs about my blunders at the yarn shop."

Sarah stood, walked to the sink, looked out the window, then turned around and studied Eunice. "So, no goosebumps or butterflies or racing heart?"

"That stuff is only in books, Sarah. Not real life."

Sarah sat back down beside her. "In a way you're right, and in a way you're wrong."

"Explain it to me."

"It's true that romance books talk about those things as if we're all swooning over one another—walking around with fast heartbeats, feeling out of breath, seeing little cupid hearts pop up here and there, feeling butterflies in our stomachs..."

Eunice couldn't help laughing, and somehow that laughter made her feel better. "I suppose I might have been expecting one or two of those things. But it was just—okay. It was a perfectly fine evening, but nothing to write home about."

"So you're right that the fairy-tale picture of being in love isn't real life. But, Eunice, when you're with the right person, when you're with the person that *Gotte* has meant for you... there are moments that feel special like that."

"Oh."

"Don't look sad. It'll happen when it's supposed to happen."

"Okay."

"But apparently not with Lester."

"Apparently not."

"Unless you wanted to give him another try? Maybe go for a second date?"

"*Nein.* I think one date with Lester was enough. To tell you the truth, I couldn't get past the idea that if we did care for each other, one of us would need to convert to the other's religion."

"That would be pretty far down the road."

"But I don't want to go down that road at all. Not now. Not six months from now. I like being Amish, and I suspect Lester enjoys being Mennonite."

"Which is one more way of saying you're not the ideal person for each other."

"Yup." And now she felt better about it. The night had been a little disappointing, and she hadn't been able to figure out why. "Talking with you always helps."

They both stood and Sarah pulled her into a hug. Eunice was suddenly aware of the child her *schweschder* was carrying and something in her heart twisted. Would she ever be a mom? Did she want to be?

Then holding Eunice at arm's length, Sarah studied her.

"What? Do I have trail mix on my face?"

"*Nein.* It's just that I love you, and you've turned into a beautiful and smart and kind woman."

"Seriously?"

"Seriously."

Now Eunice felt immeasurably better. Funny how Sarah could give you a pep talk, and you didn't even realize that was what she was doing.

As Eunice walked Sarah out to her buggy, she told her

about the tours, the guests and then finally about Zeb and how he was seeing a doctor.

"That's a big step."

"I know it. I'm proud of him."

"You two have always been close."

"Close but only friends, so don't give me that smile." Eunice thought that Sarah was practically glowing. Her baby bump was beginning to show. She was in love. She had moved on with her life—past the confines of the home she'd grown up in.

"Sometimes, what starts as friendship grows into something else."

"If you say so."

"Keep dating."

"Okay."

"It's probably going to take more than one attempt to hit the jackpot."

"Right."

As Sarah drove away, Eunice stood watching. She had irritated herself by comparing Lester to Zeb in her mind all during the date. She couldn't figure out why she was doing it. She had felt powerless to stop.

She did not think Sarah was right about friendship turning into love, at least not in this instance.

But she was probably right that it would take more than one attempt at dating to find someone special. If she was with the right guy, she wouldn't be thinking about Zeb. The only question was, who could this new romantic interest possibly be? Because she couldn't think of a single person.

Maybe it was time to ask someone else's advice.

Her family could only help her so much. She needed to ask someone who was her age and someone who knew her pretty well. And, suddenly, she knew just who that was.

Chapter Twelve

The next day was a church Sunday, and they were meeting at Bethany and Ada's farm. Eunice was looking forward to the day. She liked when church service was at a family member's place. It felt like being at home, only someone else was in charge of getting the benches set up, arranging the potluck table and all the other things that came with holding a church meeting for over a hundred people. They'd joked for years about one day needing to split into two church districts, but Eunice hoped that didn't happen anytime soon. She liked things the way they were.

Plus the house on Huckleberry Lane had grown into a very special place for the Yoder family. Ada and Ethan and Peter were now living in a smaller home that had been constructed next to the main house. Bethany, Aaron, Lydia and Daniel lived in the original house which had gone through a much-needed renovation. There was a covered breezeway between the two which made it easy to carry things back and forth between the two families during rainy weather or snowstorms.

Sunday morning dawned rainy and a bit colder. Eunice lay in bed for a few extra minutes, listening to the rain drum against the roof. The weather didn't dampen her mood at all. The temperatures were cold as they should be in mid-November, but it wasn't freezing. She dressed quickly, made a light breakfast for her and her *dat*, and they were ready to head over to the church service as Gideon, Becca, Mary and Abram stepped out of their home. Eunice loved that they'd built on the family property. She liked all of her family being close enough to drop in on, or borrow sugar from, or cry on their shoulder.

Not that she felt like crying today.

Eunice's mind was made up, and with that decision came courage.

She and her *dat* had talked about everyday things on the ride over—the weather, the recent circle letter from their family in Kentucky, the upcoming holidays. Time seemed to speed up and they were suddenly pulling into Huckleberry Lane. Eunice felt almost giddy as she hopped out of the buggy and hurried to help her *schweschdern*. They shooed her away, telling her it was all taken care of and that she should enjoy the day of worship.

The main room of the barn had been set up for services with the doors flung open to let in extra light. Even with the rain and the cool temperatures, the giant room warmed up quickly.

Eunice liked worshipping in a barn. She liked the smell of the hay, the occasional neighing of horses, the way they all sat a little closer to one another. It reminded her of being a child and playing in the barn. Those were happy memories from a time that existed after the grief of her mother's passing and before the awkwardness of adolescence. It was possible that she'd stayed in the barn all of these years for that very reason.

It felt nice.

And safe.

But Eunice had woken that morning tired of nice and safe. She couldn't explain what had changed. Was it the so-so date with Lester? The talk with Sarah? Her growing confidence due to the successful tours? Maybe her newfound confidence was a result of learning to knit. She'd actually done two rows of a hat the day before, without dropping a single stitch.

Whatever the reason, she could hardly wait for the service to begin. She was looking forward to worshipping. The hymns were some of her favorites. The preaching was on Isaiah chapter forty-one. *Be of good courage.* It was almost as if every aspect of the service was confirming that this day was the day she was meant to step out of her old life and into her new.

She managed to wait until Zeb and Josh had eaten and scraped their plates clean before excusing herself from the table where all her *schweschdern* and their families were sitting.

"Where are you off to?" Bethany asked.

"Tell you later."

"Tell you later, alligator." Ada echoed Eunice in a singsong voice, as she snuggled baby Peter. "See her smile, crocodile."

Eunice heard Peter laughing as she walked away.

She caught up with Zeb and Josh at the horse stall located at the far end of the barn. Ethan had enlarged it and made it as comfortable as possible for Ada's menagerie. Josh was already inside the stall. Zeb was standing at the half door which had been closed to keep any wayward pet from escaping. He nodded hello, then tilted his head toward Josh, who didn't seem at all surprised to look up and see her.

"Do you know this one's name, Eunice?"

"Sure. That's Pongo. He's a Boer goat."

"And is the donkey really blind?"

"We think Matilda can see shadows."

Josh had plopped onto the ground next to Matilda and was gingerly petting her between the ears. One of the beagles climbed into his lap, and he started laughing when it licked him in the face.

"And the dogs? What are their names?"

She hesitated, trying to remember which was which. The beagles looked like identical twins to her.

"Don't tell me you've forgotten the names of the dogs." Zeb's voice was low, teasing, closer than she'd realized.

Eunice tossed her *kapp* strings behind her shoulders and tried to act as if Zeb's standing so close to her didn't bother her one bit. Why was it bothering her? He was simply one of her best friends. Except today he was cleaned up, smelling nice and wearing freshly laundered clothes. If she wasn't mistaken, he'd also cut his hair.

"I know their names. That's Ginger. Or maybe Snap." She looked to the beagle curled up in the corner next to Pongo, then back at Josh. "Kinda hard to tell, actually."

"This is not a normal horse stall." Zeb crossed his arms over the half door, staring into the stall, probably trying to come up with an explanation for the strange assortment of animals. Surprisingly, he didn't seem at all perturbed or overly protective that his son sat in the midst of them.

Eunice mimicked his posture at the half door. "Before Ada went to work with the SPCA, before she and Ethan fell in love, she became an animal rescuer. That's how she accumulated all of these *lost ones*—her name for them, not mine." She hesitated for the space of a heartbeat. "Say, do you mind if I talk to you about something?"

Zeb looked surprised, but shrugged and said, "I guess."

"Okay. This is a little hard to say, so I'll plunge right in." Eunice noticed she now had his full attention, but she tried not to let that bother her. Why was she so aware of him all of a sudden? When had she felt awkward around Zeb Mast? Happy—sure. Irritated—more than once. Infuriated—yeah.

But awkward? Crossing her arms felt defensive, but dropping them at her side felt odd too.

"You were going to say…"

"Right. As you predicted, my date with Lester didn't go so well."

Zeb's shoulders stiffened. "Did he—"

"He was a perfect gentleman. He just—well, as you might have hinted, he just wasn't my type."

"Oh. Okay."

"But, and this is the embarrassing part, I realized that maybe I am ready to date. Maybe it won't be as awkward and demoralizing as when I was a *youngie*."

Zeb glanced over the stall door, seemed satisfied that Josh was okay, and lightly tugged on Eunice's arm to pull her away a few feet. "Little pitchers, big ears, and all that."

"Huh?"

"Why was dating awkward for you? Why was it demoralizing?"

"Well, Zeb, because I'm sure at least a third of the time, the guy was simply following a dare to date me."

"*Nein.* No one in our community is that cruel."

"Maybe they didn't mean to be cruel."

"When did this happen?"

"We were kids—teens, I guess. And like any other teens we didn't always do the commendable thing. I know at least one time…" She put her hands on her hips and stared at the ground, then looked up at him. "*Nein.* This doesn't embarrass me anymore. I did nothing to be embarrassed about. But at least one time, I heard someone say something like *I did it. I dated the greasy girl. Now you owe me five dollars.*"

"You were never greasy."

"I probably had oil or something under my nails. I do remember that I was already taking apart small engines. I had found something I was *gut* at, and I loved doing it. But that same hobby sort of made me a target. I guess."

"That shouldn't have happened."

"We were kids. Kids can be thoughtless. But that's not my point. My point is that we're adults now, and maybe most of us are done with those kinds of foolish games."

"Meaning what?"

"Meaning I'm ready to date again."

Zeb stared at her, his mouth slightly open, his ears reddening.

Eunice realized her mistake and rushed to assure him she wasn't trying to lay a trap for him. Gosh. He really did think women were just hanging out waiting for an instant family. "I'm not explaining this well. When I was telling Sarah about my date, she mentioned you."

Now Zeb pulled in his bottom lip and refused to look directly at her, but still he didn't speak.

"I told her, of course, that we were just friends."

"Oh." His eyes darted toward her and then away. "Right. Okay."

"But it did start me thinking that no one knows me quite like you do."

"We go back a ways."

"Exactly. So maybe you'd have a suggestion about who I should date. I mean, my *dat*, he has the best of intentions. But he doesn't really understand our age group. At least, I don't think he does."

"So you want me to set you up with someone?"

"That sounds more desperate than I'd intended. But kind of. Yes." Eunice couldn't believe she'd done it. She couldn't believe she'd been so bracingly honest with Zeb. But then he was, for all practical purposes, her best friend. If she couldn't be honest with him, then who could she be honest with?

And the fact that her heart did a little skip, like Sarah had described, well it didn't mean that she necessarily cared for Zeb in that way. It could simply mean she was nervous. Or maybe catching a cold.

Finally, Zeb nodded. "Okay. Let me think on it, but I should be able to come up with a couple of names."

"Whew."

"Whew? What did you think I was going to say?"

"Something along the lines of, 'Are you kidding? Are you sure? Have you lost your mind?'"

Now he smiled and shook his head. "You stumped me, for sure and certain, but I can tell you're not kidding. And you seem to be sure this is what you want to do. You seem to have thought this out. Which means you haven't lost your mind."

She nodded, satisfied with his answer, and walked back to the stall door. Josh was now lying on his back, with a beagle pressed up against each side. "He's a good kid," she said.

"Yeah, he is."

"How's your counseling thing going?"

"*Gut.* I guess. I mean, I only go once a week, so I haven't been back since you and I talked…but I think it's helping."

"That's great, Zeb. I'm truly glad to hear it."

"Want to hear something funny?"

"Ha-ha funny or sad funny?"

"Probably the second one." He lowered his voice, even turned his back so that his words wouldn't reach Josh. "I remember thinking, not so long ago, that you were the smart one because you hadn't fallen in love. You hadn't risked everything and then lost it."

She watched him closely, trying to understand the meaning behind his words. Zeb was going through something. She was hoping it was a good thing, but was worried it might be bad.

"That sounds a little…bitter."

"Yup."

"And not at all like *Do Not Fear*."

"I was listening to the sermon, and again—you're probably right."

"Which means we both are still learning, still growing. That's a good thing."

"It is." He looked at her fully now, studied her, didn't rush or speak or pretend he needed to do something else. And his full attention made her feel as if a dozen butterflies had been released in her stomach. It made her feel…seen.

Josh hopped up, claiming if he didn't have a cookie soon he might actually die.

Zeb cleared his throat, stepped back and said, "I'll get you some names."

But there was something in the way he said it that made Eunice think he wasn't entirely on board with her plan. And she had no idea why.

Zeb was continually surprised at how much Josh heard and understood. No matter what he was doing, or how distracted he appeared, the boy always seemed to pick up on what was being said around him. To Zeb, it often looked as if his son's attention was a million miles away. Like today, when he'd been so excited about Ada's animals. And yet, apparently he had still heard every word that passed between Zeb and Eunice.

How did Zeb know that? As Samuel drove home, with Zeb sitting beside him and Joshua in the back seat, Josh brought up his conversation with Eunice.

In fact, he leaned over the front seat and said, "You're finding a date for Eunice?"

Samuel nearly drove the buggy off the road. Beauty tossed her head and maneuvered back into the middle of the lane.

"Sorry, girl," Samuel said to the mare. Then he shot Zeb a look. "Is that true?"

"Pretty much."

"Want to explain that to me?"

"Not much to explain really. Eunice said she'd been on a date with Lester…" Even he realized he'd said the name as if he were describing a snake in the grass. "He was apparently not her type."

"That's what she said?"

"Yup. I heard her." Josh put his hands on the back of the seat and his chin on his hands. "I don't understand why anyone would want to date. I mean, kissing and stuff? Gross."

"Give it a few years, Josh. You'll change your opinion on that."

"Hopefully more than a few," Zeb murmured.

"We both like Eunice. In fact, I think she's swell. Why don't *you* just ask her out, *Dat*? That would be way easier."

"Ya, *bruder*. Why don't *you* just ask her out?"

Zeb was surprised to find he wasn't as irritated by this conversation as he might have been a week ago. "She didn't ask to go out with me," he explained. "She asked for the names of one or two guys who I thought would be a good match for her."

Samuel's mouth was now open wide enough to catch an autumn leaf. Josh had fallen back against his seat. "Eunice is cool and all. I like seeing how she takes stuff apart and puts it all back again. But if I ever like a girl in a smoochy way—"

"A smoochy way?"

Josh made a loud kissing sound. "Don't look so worried. I don't. I'm only five! But if I ever do, it's going to be because she has a lot of animals, like Ada. Wouldn't that be amazing? You could have a best girl and a blind goat. Just think of it."

Zeb was happy when Samuel turned the conversation to other things, but as they were unharnessing Beauty, after Josh had gone inside to clean up before dinner, Samuel couldn't help returning to the subject.

"She likes you. That's why she asked you, Zeb. Josh wasn't so far off. You should have asked her out."

"I didn't get that feeling at all." Though now that he thought of it, she had blushed prettily. Still, that could have been from embarrassment due to the topic. It probably was from embarrassment. "It took a lot of courage for her to ask for help with dating."

"Why now?"

"She said the date with Lester made her realize she's ready, but that he's not the guy."

"Okay. And why did she ask you?"

"Because we're good friends."

Samuel led Beauty to her stall as Zeb made sure everything in the barn was put in its proper place. They walked out of the barn into a perfect November afternoon—rainy but perfect. What farmer didn't like rain? And he still thought of himself as a farmer, even if the money from the tours was quickly outpacing what he made from crops.

As they were walking up the steps to the house, Samuel said, "Sometimes a girl doesn't know how to say she likes you. Sometimes she asks a different question."

"That doesn't even make sense."

"Sure it does. Remember that story *Mamm* told us? She'd asked *Dat* to come over and help her with a washing machine, when what she really wanted was an excuse to spend time with him."

"Okay. I guess that's true sometimes, but I'm not sure it's true in this case."

"So, you're just going to set Eunice up with someone else?"

"I don't know. I'm going to think on it. I told her I'd give her some names."

"I'll tell you what you should do. Get a piece of paper and write one name on it. Write your name on it, and then take the woman on a proper date."

Samuel bumped his shoulder against Zeb's, and for a moment it felt like they were *youngies*, talking about which girl at school they liked. Zeb was only twenty-five years old, but when he thought about his younger self… When he thought about how carefree he'd been, it seemed as if that was a different person.

Later that night, he sat in the living room writing in his journal. It still felt awkward, but the counselor had insisted that it would help him process his feelings. What he'd learned since starting that practice was that feelings were messy. Often his feelings one day contradicted his feelings the next day. Many times he didn't understand what he felt at all, but he was learning to accept those things about himself.

He wrote about the day, then about the story his *mamm* had told him before moving. The story about her broken heart and how it had taken awhile before she was ready to love again.

What if she'd never done that?

What if she'd never stepped out in courage after being hurt?

She wouldn't have married their *dat*.

He and Samuel wouldn't exist. Josh wouldn't exist.

His pen froze over the paper. What he'd said to Eunice had been true. He had thought that not falling in love might be preferable to the pain he'd endured the last two years. But if he hadn't fallen in love, he wouldn't have Josh.

And there was something else his *mamm* had said.

He doodled on the side of the page, trying to remember her exact words. And when he was sure he had it right, he wrote it in the journal.

Sometimes love looks different the second time around.

Chapter Thirteen

Eunice didn't expect to hear from Zeb until Wednesday at the earliest, since that was their first tour of the week. So she was super surprised when he walked into The Stitch & Skein around lunchtime on Tuesday.

"Zeb, what are you doing here?"

"Thought I'd pick up some yarn."

He said it so casually that she couldn't help laughing.

"Didn't take you for a knitter, but okay. Can I help you pick something out?"

Zeb jerked his head toward the opposite side of the store. She followed him and couldn't help quipping, "Didn't realize organic yarn was your thing."

"Huh?"

She pointed to the organic merino wool sign and the display beneath it.

"I don't know what that means."

"Which is fine, since you're not a knitter. Why are you here?"

"To ask you out."

Eunice had been straightening the red organic merino yarn, but her hands froze, her mind froze, at Zeb's words. She turned to face him, to see if he was serious.

"I know that's not what you asked for. You asked for a list of names."

"*Ya.*"

"Samuel said I should give you a piece of paper with my name on it, but that sounded kind of corny."

"Samuel said that?"

"Josh was even in on it. Saying kissing was gross, but since Ada was taken I should ask you…" His words slowed and trickled to an end with, "Or something like that."

"You're asking me to go out on a date? With you?"

He'd been reaching out to touch a skein of yarn, but he jerked his hand back, stuck it in his pocket and stood up straighter. "I am, Eunice. I'd like to take you out later this week. If that works for you."

Did it work for her?

Did she want to date Zeb?

"I suspect you're thinking the same thing I am," he said.

"And what's that?"

"We could be messing up a good friendship, a friendship that's important to both of us. But…" He shook his head. "Something about this feels right. Don't you think? And if I'm wrong, then we'll go back to the way we've been."

"Huh."

"Is that a yes?"

And suddenly she could hear Ada's voice. *See her smile, crocodile.* Ada's misquotes and Ada's sweet heart. Maybe Ada had been right all along. Maybe Eunice had been taking life, taking everything entirely too seriously.

She pushed any reservations or questions away, and she said what her heart told her to say. "Yes."

"Tomorrow after the tour? I already checked with Becca and she said she wouldn't mind keeping Josh a few extra hours."

"You spoke with Becca?"

Zeb nodded. "Wanted to have my ducks in a row."

"Okay. Tomorrow after the tour then. Where are we going?"

Zeb smiled, and it was the first genuine smile she'd seen from her friend in a very long time. "I'll figure something out."

Eunice wasn't a very good employee at the shop after that. She stocked cotton yarn in the wool section, refilled an entire display of craft books upside down and charged a customer $112.49 instead of $12.49.

"That would be quite expensive yarn." The customer laughed good-humoredly as Myra rushed over to help her correct the error.

When they were alone again in the shop, Myra turned to her and said, "You've got the lovebug."

"What?"

"You heard me. It's all over your face." Myra held up her hands and made circles in the air—as if she were washing a window. "Love struck."

"No, I'm not."

"Okay. If you say so. But something changed when that nice young man came in and asked you out."

"You heard that?"

"Small shop. I couldn't help but hear."

"I'm sorry I'm so distracted." Eunice pressed her palms to her cheeks. She needed a cold rag. She felt as if her face were on fire.

Myra patted her shoulder. "There, there." She actually said those words. Had anyone ever said *there, there* to Eunice before?

"Why don't you take off early today? Maybe take a little drive. The weather's cleared. It's a beautiful crisp, cool, autumn day."

"But I still haven't—"

"We'll take care of those things tomorrow. Go on, now. Get your purse. Are you okay to drive the buggy?"

"Of course I'm okay to drive the buggy. Why wouldn't I be?"

"Go home. Have a little rest. Maybe take a walk. Walks are good for the lovelorn."

"But I'm not—"

"Yup. So you say." Myra walked her through the store-room. As Eunice was leaving out the back door, Myra pulled her into a hug. "I know it's all confusing, dear. But falling *in lieb* is *wunderbaar*. For many people it only happens once in a lifetime. Try to enjoy it."

Eunice walked over to her buggy in something of a daze. She spoke to the mare. "How about a drive, Peanut?" And she did feel better once the cool air was on her face and the sound of Peanut's clip-clop filled the afternoon.

She didn't realize where she was going until she pulled into Sarah's drive. Her husband, Noah, had served time in an Illinois state prison. He was a new man now, and he loved Sarah so much that it sometimes hurt Eunice to watch the two of them together. Sarah and Noah had moved in with his parents. Though the house was small and the acreage enough for a single man to work alone, they'd wanted to be together.

Noah's parents had missed him terribly the years he'd been in Illinois. When Noah and Sarah had married, Eunice hadn't been able to imagine Sarah living anywhere but their home. Now, though, as she pulled up to the house and saw Sarah hanging clothes on the line, she knew that this was where Sarah belonged.

How did something like that happen?

How did a life take a completely different direction?

And was it possible for her?

She helped hang the laundry, and then they took a long walk. Sarah listened to her worries and her fears and her hopes. She didn't laugh. She didn't correct. She listened.

Eunice's oldest *schweschder* had always been a very *gut* listener.

By the time they were back at the house, Noah's *mamm*, Rachel, was sitting on the front porch with three glasses and a pitcher of lemonade. They sat in the rockers enjoying the fall weather. Sarah told the story of her first date with Noah, back before she'd really known anything about him. Back when Noah was afraid to reveal his past.

Rachel told them that she'd met Reuben, Noah's *dat*, at a work day. He'd come over from Middlebury to help with a barn raising. "It was love at first sight," she admitted. "And I didn't believe in such a thing."

It helped Eunice to hear these women's stories. It helped to know that it was normal to feel confused and scared and excited all at the same time.

But what carried her through the next twenty-four hours was Sarah's words as they were walking over to the buggy. Sarah looped her arm through Eunice's. "Zeb is a *gut* friend to you, Eunice. And he might be more. But if this doesn't work out, you'll still be friends."

"Can you promise me that?"

"*Ya.* I can, actually. It might be awkward at first. You might blush or feel silly around one another, but then that will pass. You and Zeb will always be friends. *Gotte* put you in this place, here in our little Shipshe, at the same time so that you could support one another. Whether or not that friendship turns into something else…" She pulled Eunice into a hug. "Time will tell."

What Sarah said was something that Eunice could believe because she wanted with all of her heart for it to be true.

Zeb thought he'd be nervous. It had been a long time since he'd been alone with a woman. But this was Eunice. After going over his options for afternoon dates with Samuel, he'd called and left a message for Eunice to dress comfortably.

But when he arrived at the Yoder farm with the tour guests, he couldn't tell that she'd worn an older dress. Eunice looked nice in whatever she had on. He'd once seen her in a pair of overalls that she'd picked up at a thrift store. They were just out of school then—only fourteen years old. Eunice had been trying to take apart the engine of an old Ford pickup that someone had towed to her place. When he'd stopped by, she'd been covered with grease and determined to make that old Ford run again. She'd been successful too, though soon after she'd decided that her talent was more for small engines.

She looked every bit as lovely today as she had then.

The tour went well. The guests laughed at Eunice's jokes, had plenty of questions for her, and enjoyed Becca's afternoon snack—which included Sarah's new blend of granola. Nearly every guest purchased at least one quart jar of it, and many purchased several.

Once the *Englischers* had piled back into Martin's retrofitted school bus, Becca shooed them away.

"Go, go on your date. Josh and Mary are playing Connect 4. He'll be fine here."

So they'd gone. Zeb felt like a teenager sneaking out after dark. He felt as if he was getting away with something. In fact, what he was doing was claiming a few hours of the day for himself. When was the last time he'd done that?

He and Eunice chatted about the tourists, the upcoming holiday and the Christmas parade, which was in a couple of days. The parade was always held on the Friday before Thanksgiving. He could tell that it was one of Eunice's favorite Shipshe celebrations. She described the lights, the food, even the music.

"It's grown a little since we were *youngies*."

"I was here last year, you know."

"You were here, but you weren't—" She stopped, apparently at a loss of words.

"I know what you mean. I probably wouldn't have noticed if there'd been a giraffe pulling Santa's sleigh." All he could really remember of the previous year was an overwhelming sense of darkness. He still felt it, at times, but it no longer seemed to cover every moment of every day. "Josh remembers last year's parade. I think my parents went with us. He's been talking about it all week. He especially loves how the houses and businesses on the route turn off their lights."

"Makes the candles and flashlights everyone is holding seem like stars in the sky."

"Exactly."

When he pulled into the parking lot for The Cove, Eunice looked at him in surprise. "We're going to play volleyball?"

"Not exactly."

Stopping at Shipshe's community center had been Samuel's idea. The building was mainly a youth center, but Samuel had assured him that there wasn't a definitive age limit. The facility itself had been built in 2015. All necessary costs were covered by donations. The area's three thousand Amish *youngies* played volleyball, basketball, chess, cornhole and more recently—pickleball.

Samuel had insisted it would make for a great first date. He'd assured him that pickleball would be simple to learn to play and claimed it would help with their nerves. The Cove had eight pickleball courts, and six of them were open. Eunice and Zeb took the court farthest away from the other players, in case their balls went wild. There were pickleball rules posted on the wall next to the court.

Eunice studied the rules sheet. "Let's see. 'Stay out of the kitchen.'"

"Where's the kitchen?" Zeb squinted at the photograph, then peered over at their court.

"It's this part." Eunice tapped the rules sheet, trying not to laugh. "The part near the net. The non-volley zone. You can't go there."

"Oh. Okay." Zeb was already itching to get on the court. He used to love to play badminton and he'd even played a little tennis. This looked like a combination of the two. "We play to eleven. Have to win by two."

"Looks like a tennis court," Eunice noted.

"Yeah. Balls and racquets are different though."

"Paddles." Eunice gave him a challenging grin. "Let's just give it a try. How bad can we be?"

Turned out they were pretty bad. Zeb kept forgetting and trying to serve as if he were playing tennis, which didn't work well at all. Twice Eunice hit the ball before it bounced, which caused Zeb to laugh out loud and claim the point. They dove and ran and lunged and laughed. Zeb was surprised when the courts around them started filling up.

"We've been at it an hour," Eunice said. "That's more exercise than chasing my nieces and nephews."

They gave up their court to a group of four that looked barely old enough to be out of school.

"Should have watched some others before we tried to play."

"Bested by someone ten years younger?" Eunice shook her head in mock wonder. "Who would have thought it possible?"

"It doesn't seem like we played for an hour."

"Time literally flew by while I was chasing a wiffle ball."

"Did you enjoy it?" Zeb asked.

"I did. You?"

"Yup. Stopped my brain for a few minutes."

"That's a *gut* thing?"

"Yes. Apparently, I overthink things."

They stopped at the Blue Gate Restaurant for pie and coffee.

"I don't come in here very often," Eunice admitted.

"Same."

"It's very nice."

"It is."

"And this pie." Eunice leaned forward waving a forkful of fresh strawberry at him. "It might be better than Sarah's, but don't tell her I said so."

He leaned toward her, Eunice gave up the piece of pie, and as she plopped it in his mouth their eyes met. Something inside of Zeb came unbound in that moment. Some emotion that he hadn't let himself feel, hadn't let himself even think about, and now he was flooded by it.

Appreciation? Fondness? Love?

He couldn't love Eunice Yoder. They'd been on one date. Of course, he'd known her all his life. And Eunice had been there for him since the day he'd returned to Shipshe. Even when he'd been rude and blamed her for Josh's accident.

The question was, did he want her to be more?

As they walked back to the buggy, it occurred to Zeb that this was like the old days. It felt natural to be with Eunice. She was a *gut* friend. How was this even a date? He was simply hanging out with someone that he liked. There was no need to make it into something that it wasn't.

But then Eunice stopped to pick up a golden leaf that had fallen next to his buggy. She held it up for him to see, a smile lighting up her face. Zeb had carefully planned the date, if that was what this was. He'd taken Samuel's advice, picked something active and then taken Eunice to a nice place for a snack.

"Not dinner," Samuel had said. "Dinner is serious and comes with a lot of pressure. Neither of you need that."

What he and Samuel had decided on had been the right thing. The plan had gone beautifully. But what he did next wasn't in the plan. Eunice stepped closer, the smile still dancing in her eyes, as she held the leaf out for him to examine.

But he wasn't looking at the maple leaf.

He was looking at Eunice and seeing her in a new light. He stepped closer, lowered his head and kissed her softly. When he stepped back, she remained where she was. Had he messed up?

The smile returned, and she laughed softly.

"What?"

"Never figured you for a good kisser."

"Oh, is that right?"

"Just saying."

On the ride home, he didn't have to sneak a peek one time at the topics he'd written on the palm of his hand. They talked about their childhood memories that centered around the upcoming holidays, how he planned to celebrate with Josh, how the Yoder house would be filled with *grandkinner*.

"This was nice," Eunice said, as they walked up Becca's front porch steps.

"Care to repeat today's experiment?"

"Another game of pickleball?"

"Actually, I thought maybe you'd enjoy going to the Christmas parade with me and Joshua."

She tilted her head and studied him. He thought maybe she was trying to see if he was ready for this. But he was ready. He reached for her hand, squeezed it, and Eunice said softly, "Yes. I'd like that."

On the ride home, Josh was too busy telling him about a game he and Mary had made up—it centered around a fort they'd built in the hall, an inside game of tag and snack time.

"It was like the Olympics, in a way."

"What do you know about the Olympics, son?"

"Well. Not much. But isn't there a sport where they do several things at once?"

"Do you mean the pentathlon?" Zeb wondered where in the world Josh would have heard about that. "It's several separate events, including fencing, swimming and equestrian."

"Right. I think Old Tom was watching a YouTube video on his phone about it, while he was waiting for the tour people to come out of Becca's house one day."

"Hmm."

"Our game was like that but different. You had to make your way through the tunnel. That was the fort. Then run outside, touch the porch railing, run back inside to the table where you sit and eat your snack without spilling anything. And finally you end up back at the beginning of the tunnel. It was fun, *Dat*. We should try it at home."

Zeb reached over and tussled Josh's hair. The boy's laughter was soft, joyful, natural. And why wouldn't it be? He'd spent an afternoon playing with his friend. He'd enjoyed being a boy and not worrying about adult things.

Pulling into their lane, their conversation turned to dinner and winter and how much snow it took to build a snowman. Together they unharnessed Beauty from the buggy, groomed her and fed her. When they were walking to the house, Josh asked, "So are you going to ask Eunice out on another date?"

The question caught Zeb by surprise.

He'd thought maybe his son had forgotten where he'd gone that afternoon. But Josh was observant, and now he was watching his *dat* closely.

"Actually, we are going out again."

"Oh. That's cool. So I'll go back and play with Mary?"

"Nope. You and me and Eunice are going to the Christmas parade together."

"Seriously?"

"Seriously." Zeb slapped Josh's upheld palm.

Josh ran inside to share the news with Samuel. At dinner, Zeb told them about the pickleball game, which was even funnier in the retelling.

"Sounds like I should go with you next time, *bruder*. The game isn't that hard. You just need someone who has played it before."

"All right. If you can find a date."

To which, Samuel laughed and said, "Not a problem."

As Zeb wrote in his journal that night, he realized that he was feeling something he hadn't felt since before Suzanne's illness. He was feeling joy. Happiness. Hope. The question was whether he dared to believe it might last.

Chapter Fourteen

Eunice wasn't sure what she expected of a second date, never having been on a second date before.

"You're kidding. Right?" Bethany had stopped by to drop off freshly baked bread and a casserole dish filled with chicken potpie.

"We're not starving here. Why does everyone keep bringing food?"

"Because you have two jobs and you're dating."

"That sounds as if I have a full dance card."

"You have a dance card?" Bethany's eyes twinkled as she took baby Daniel from Eunice and propped him in her lap, then pulled a bottle from her large purse that doubled as a diaper bag.

"Nope. I don't. In fact, I'm pretty sure I don't know how to dance."

"Imagine that. So tell me all about your first date."

"I told Becca. I guess I figured she'd tell Ada and Ada would tell you."

"She did. They both did. But I want to hear it from you."

"Gotcha." So Eunice went through the entire date again. Each time she told the pickleball story, it was funnier than the time before. But the kiss. How was she supposed to describe that?

"It sounds as if you like him." Bethany put the baby up on her shoulder and proceeded to rub his back in gentle circles.

"I do. It's…it's all rather sudden and more than a little bit scary."

"You're afraid it will ruin your friendship."

"I suppose."

"Instead of worrying about what might go wrong, focus on what might go right. Just think of it, sis. If you two do fall in love, then you might marry. And if you marry, you might have a *wunderbaar* little boy like this." She turned Daniel to face her.

Eunice thought he was the most perfect baby boy she'd ever seen.

"Or a *wunderbaar* little girl like me." Lydia popped into the room. She walked over to Eunice, put her arms around her and asked, "Is it true? Are you going to get married and have babies? Because this family has a lot of them already, but I wouldn't mind more cousins."

Eunice shrugged, which was enough of an answer for Lydia.

Later that night, she sat on the front porch, wrapped in an old quilt and studying the stars. Her *dat* brought out two mugs of herbal tea and sank into the rocker beside hers. Eunice had always been close to her father, maybe more than the normal young girl since he was her only parent. There had never been difficulty between them. She'd never snuck out in the middle of the night or insisted on dating the wrong kind of guy. They'd agreed on most everything, other than his worries over her being single.

But since Sarah had married and moved out, Eunice had felt closer to her father than ever before. She appreciated his silence. She loved that he didn't push a subject or try to coax a person into talking about a thing.

Which, for Eunice, helped to loosen her tongue.

She found herself telling him about the date, though she omitted the part about the kiss. "I don't know why I'm thinking so seriously about this. It's only one date. It isn't as if we're promised to one another."

"First dates can be very important. Also, it sounds to me like you've made a turn in your journey."

"What does that mean?"

Amos laughed softly. "Life is a journey, *ya*?"

"I suppose."

"The Good Book says as much."

Eunice must have given him a skeptical look, because Amos began ticking off examples on his fingers. "We are told about the journey of Abraham, Moses and the prophets."

"True."

"And what of Job's journey? Now there's a book worth studying."

"It's a bit sad."

"And beautiful—sometimes the two go hand in hand. Then we have the life of Christ and the journeys of the disciples."

"Okay. Okay. You win. Lots of stuff about journeys there. But how is dating a journey?"

"Two ways I think. It's a journey inward." He tapped his heart.

That simple gesture reminded Eunice of his heart troubles a few years before. She'd never thought of him as vulnerable before, but weren't they all? Life was fleeting and precious.

"When we journey inward we learn about ourselves, what things are important to us, what we appreciate and like about someone else. But dating is also an outward journey, *toward* another person and also with the other person. It's a very exciting time, Eunice. I'm glad you're having this experience."

"But I don't even know how it will turn out."

"When we're the one on the journey, we never do know how it will turn out." He nodded, sipping his tea. She could just make out the silhouette of him from the beam of the lantern light in the living room.

He was aging. It hurt her to think about that. She loved her *dat* very much. But she supposed that aging, too, was a part of each of their journeys.

"*Gotte* will guide you." His voice was soft, confident, warm. "Your family—we're all here to support you, regardless which way your relationship with Zeb goes. It isn't about a pressure for things to turn out a certain way. It's more about discovering what *Gotte* has in store for your future. And that, Eunice, is a very exciting time."

She continued sitting there long after her father went inside. The night was cold, but she was warm wrapped in the old quilt that Sarah had made for her when she'd turned ten. How was it that a blanket could warm your body but a quilt could warm your body and your soul?

She slept well that night, her dreams filled with fields of ripe corn and laughter as she ran her hands along the stalks.

The sun rose over a crisp November day in northern Indiana. Amos had suggested they not have tours during the Christmas parade. Everyone was excited about the community event and wanted to participate. Eunice rode into Shipshe with Becca and Gideon. Her father was already there, having worked at the market most of the day. When she saw Zeb standing in the market's parking area, waving as if he was afraid she wouldn't see him, something in her heart soared.

Her family loved her dearly.

Her *schweschdern* were her best friends.

But when had someone looked so excited to see her? As soon as she climbed out of the buggy, Josh threw himself at her, wrapping his arms around her and giving her a gigantic hug before dancing away and saying, "We are going to find the best seats ever!"

Before she could respond, he dashed off to see Mary and Lydia.

Zeb simply reached for her hand. "Ready?"

"Oh, *ya*. I believe I am."

And then her *schweschdern* and *bruders*-in-law and nieces and nephews and even her father, they all walked together, out to the main road, jostling and laughing. Eunice realized in that moment that one significant thing had changed in her journey. She no longer felt on the outside of things.

She no longer felt like the odd woman out. She knew that it didn't take falling in love to feel like a part of a group. No, this went deeper. She'd purposely kept herself apart from others, maybe because she was shy or maybe because she was uncertain how to express herself in a group. Now, though, she felt no need to express herself or fit in.

And so she did. She smiled, showing she was feeling warm and content. She laughed. She scooched in with the group, Zeb on one side, Ada on the other. Eunice joined the others as they all clapped and whistled and cheered the floats that came down the road spreading their message of the sacred season.

Eunice thought that maybe it was a perfect night.

Maybe even better than their first date had been.

And she reveled in this new and exciting time in her life.

Zeb insisted on driving her home, though she could have ridden with a family member. Josh had fallen asleep in the back seat. When they turned into the lane, he called softly to the mare so that she stopped well before they reached the house. Turning to her, he said, "I care about you very much, Eunice." And then he'd gently, sweetly kissed her again.

And Eunice was willing to believe that this was the real thing. That Zeb was the man she'd been waiting for. She walked up the porch steps in something of a daze. *It was only a second date.* That's what she told herself as she said good night to her father, made her way upstairs, prepared for bed. But when she fell into another deep sleep, she was again in the field of corn, and this time she wasn't alone.

Zeb had the feeling that things were moving quickly. It was only a few weeks ago that his *mamm* had suggested he see a doctor. He'd taken Eunice out a total of four times now, if you included the Christmas parade, which he did. Four times did not sound like very much, but it seemed as if he'd known Eunice forever. He had known her nearly all of his life. And these new feelings—they felt right.

She was a bright woman. Kind. Beautiful.

Josh liked her—that was as plain as could be.

Zeb thought he might be falling in love. Could that even be possible? Was he betraying Suzanne? Was he sure? He wasn't sure. So after the church service on Sunday, he sought out Ezekiel in order to have a few moments alone with the man.

The day was cold, but bright and sunny. They walked around the little pond behind the house on Huckleberry Lane. Since both Ethan and Aaron lived on the property, they hosted church services twice. It felt right to be back there again. This place—this family—was beginning to feel like home.

"Those King *bruders* have made a nice home, ya?"

"They have. Ethan and Aaron seem quite content."

"Married to Bethany and Ada and three children between them." There was a mischievous glint in Ezekiel's eyes. "*Gotte* is good."

"All the time," Zeb said—the words automatic. It was something their community said. But he realized it was also something he believed. God was good. God had been good to him when He'd directed his path to merge with Suzanne's, which had brought them Joshua. And now his path was going a different way.

"But it wasn't always easy for Ethan and Aaron. They'll tell you about their family, what they went through with their parents. Times were hard when they were young and even when they became adults. They weren't sure that they could give a woman the things she needed or the things they felt she deserved."

"It's something I struggle with myself."

"Is it now?" Ezekiel nodded as if he weren't a bit surprised. "Doubt is okay, Zeb. It's natural to have doubts. But in Christ we can have confidence."

"It's Josh I'm worried about. Will my feelings for Eunice confuse him?"

"Have you asked?"

"*Nein.* I haven't. Seems a heavy topic for a five-year-old."

"And yet, it's important to share what's in your heart, in a way that he will understand."

"Right."

They were at the far side of the pond now. Zeb could just make out the group moving in and out of the barn. He supposed the parents were checking on children, the children were playing games of tag, the *youngies* looked to be attempting a game of softball in the field though it was probably too cold for that.

"What else is on your mind?"

"Josh. Josh is always on my mind. Am I parenting him as I should? Would marrying again be the right move for him? Would he adjust to Eunice being his new *mamm*, and before you ask… I have not asked her. We've only been on four dates. Why am I even thinking this way? It seems too soon. Too fast."

"Perhaps your thoughts are catching up with your heart."

"Maybe."

"May I speak frankly?" Ezekiel asked.

Ezekiel was the only bishop that Zeb had ever really known. The bishop in Lancaster was someone that he'd been polite to, but never really become close with. He'd never had a heart-to-heart discussion like this. Ezekiel had married Zeb's parents. He'd probably been present at Zeb's birth. He'd always been frank.

But Zeb nodded as if he were taking the question seriously. "*Ya, ya.* Of course you can."

"*Gotte* has chosen you to raise this boy, Zeb. It's a precious job—a higher calling. You can trust that *Gotte* will also equip you to do this very hard thing. He's started already, by filling you with an unmeasurable love for Joshua."

Zeb nodded, though a lump in his throat prevented him from speaking.

"Pray on this. Don't be afraid to ask *Gotte* for His direction. Pray about Eunice, about your feelings for her, about your concern for Josh. You'll know the right thing to do."

It was exactly what Zeb needed to hear.

That night he spoke to Josh, told him that he cared for Eunice, asked for his opinion on their dating.

Josh said simply, "*Ya.* Cool." Then he preceded to knock over his glass of milk and refuse to eat his vegetables. The first was an accident of course, the second not so much.

On Wednesday, he broke a vase in Becca's house.

"You were told not to play ball inside, Josh."

"*Ya*, but it's always raining outside."

The weather had turned. The temperatures were cold, but

not cold enough to freeze the roads. The rain was constant and much drearier than a week of snow would have been.

On Thursday, Josh woke in a bad mood, refusing to cooperate at all with anything that Zeb asked him to do.

By Friday, he had a meltdown in the buggy on the way to Becca's home. Zeb couldn't cancel the tour, but he didn't feel good leaving his son with Becca.

"We'll be fine. Maybe he can rest and read a book."

He didn't rest, and he didn't read a book. Instead, he snuck outside and refused to come in when called. Apparently, he'd been hiding behind the chicken coop.

"I don't know what's going on with him," Zeb admitted to Eunice.

"Well. Maybe it's normal for a boy his age."

"Maybe. He acted this way after Suzanne died."

"Is it coming up on the anniversary?"

"*Nein.* She passed in March."

"Has anything else changed?"

They were once again standing in the kitchen as Becca served the guests hot drinks and cookies. It felt natural for him to be here with Eunice. It felt right.

"I tried to talk to him about us."

"About us?" Her eyes widened. She stared at him, waiting, unable or unwilling to say the words for him.

"About how we feel about each other. At least, how I think we feel about each other."

"Well—" Her cheeks flushed, and a smile tugged at the corners of her mouth. "I've enjoyed our dates."

"But it feels like something more. Right? I'm not the only one who feels like this is going very fast?"

"This?"

"Our relationship. We seem to have gone from friends to…well, to something more in a very short amount of time."

Eunice cleared her throat. "Sarah says it's different for different people."

"You've spoken to her? About us?"

"Yeah. I have."

He reached for her hand, squeezed it, thought of kissing her. Which of course was when one of the tourists walked in looking for a refill on the coffee. Eunice helped him, and Zeb went in search of Josh who was supposed to be in Mary's room but wasn't. He finally found him in the buggy, lying in the back seat, throwing a tennis ball against the ceiling.

"Son, I've been calling you for twenty minutes."

"Oh. Couldn't hear you."

"Couldn't or didn't want to?"

"What's the difference?"

"We'll talk about this more when we get home."

"Whatever."

Zeb felt as if he were talking to an antagonistic teenager. His son was five. Where had all of this attitude come from?

He spoke with Eunice on the phone the next day. "It pains me to say it, but perhaps we should put our dating on hold."

"Okay."

It was hard to guess exactly what she was thinking from one word. So, he asked. "Is it okay? Are you okay with this?"

"Zeb, I care about you and about Joshua. If Joshua needs time to process what is going on between you and me, then let's give him time."

They decided to take a break for the rest of December. Zeb didn't like it, but he honestly didn't know what else to do. He received word that his loan had been approved. The first thing he did was call Eunice at the yarn shop. She congratulated him, and he admitted how relieved he was. But the knowledge that he'd be able to raise Josh in his childhood home didn't bring him the joy he would have expected.

Did the place really matter? Or was it the people that made a place special? When he wrote in his journal, he admitted to himself that he'd been picturing Eunice there, sharing their life. And now, he didn't know if that was going to happen.

Christmas wasn't the joyous affair he'd imagined. He spent it at home with Samuel and Josh. The boy's mood seemed to brighten when he opened his gifts. A ball and glove from Samuel. Newly knitted mittens, hat and scarf from Zeb's parents. A book about farm animals from Zeb.

Then Christmas was over.

A week later, Zeb put the new calendar on the wall hook in the kitchen—where his *mamm* had always kept it.

He would still see Eunice at the tours that were set to begin again the next week. Would that make things better or worse?

He wasn't sure he'd done the right thing.

He wasn't happy that he'd put his relationship with Eunice on hold. And going into the new year, he had absolutely no idea what he'd done wrong with his son or how he could possibly fix it. But he did know that he needed Eunice in this new year. He didn't want to even attempt it on his own.

How could he be sensitive to whatever Josh was going through and still hold true to his dreams, to the love he felt for Eunice?

And how long would she be willing to wait?

Chapter Fifteen

As Zeb walked back to the parked buggy where Josh was supposed to be waiting, his irritation grew. He'd plainly told the boy to wait on the bench in front of the horse. But was he there? Nope. The bench was empty.

Zeb thought that he should probably be more strict.

His son needed to learn to follow simple directions.

When he reached the buggy and the horse and the empty bench, Zeb stood there, hands on hips, turning in a circle. Josh wasn't in the nearby playground. He wasn't in the buggy or the parking lot. He wasn't in the picnic area. Getting down on his hands and knees, he looked under the buggy. No Josh there. Then he looked inside the buggy again. Still no Josh.

"Where did he go, Beauty?"

The mare simply nodded her head. She didn't offer a single clue. The sky had turned darker and a soft rain was beginning to fall. There was no one to ask, so Zeb did the only thing left to do. He stood there, in the rain, hollering to the north, then the east, south and west.

He slipped his hands into his pockets, then pulled them out again. Plucked his hat off his head. Hollered, "Josh. Where are you, son? Time to come back."

No response. Only silence and the drip drip drip of rain slapping against the leaves of the trees, the top of the buggy, the pavement. January and it was still raining. When would it change to snow? And where was his son?

Zeb began to sweat, though the day was cool. He didn't know what else to do. He didn't know where else to look. Panic was trying to claw its way up his spine and into his heart. He needed to remain calm.

So, he opened the door of the buggy, and that was when he saw the half sheet of paper torn from his son's drawing tablet. Scribbled there in Josh's painstaking handwriting were words that catapulted Zeb past panic and into terror.

Goin away dont look 4 me

He stared at the words, blinked, wiped water from his eyes and read them again. Had Josh run away? This could not mean that Josh had run away. He closed his eyes and tried to remember what he'd said to the boy on leaving. Something along the lines of, "Stay here and stay out of trouble for once."

He'd been tired, running behind, frustrated.

And he'd taken it out on his five-year-old son.

He hopped out of the buggy. Beauty was sheltered under a tree for the most part, and the rain was still light. The mare would be fine. He started running back toward the market. No one was there, and it was nearly dark. Where would Josh have gone?

"Josh. Come out, son."

Maybe the boy thought he was playing a game. Maybe this was nothing more than an exaggerated game of hide and seek.

Goin away dont look 4 me

Where would he have gone? Zeb practically ran to the market's offices, which were closed up and locked. Everyone had left hours ago. A few minutes earlier, he had used his own key to unlock the front door of the building and leave the tour money on Amos's desk.

Had Josh followed him?

Maybe slipped into the office building?

Zeb once again entered the building. He moved quickly up and down the halls. Calling Josh's name. Looking for small wet shoe prints. His heart rate was accelerated, and he was sweating again. He'd lost his son. How had he managed to lose his son?

First his wife and now...

His mind shied away from the thought. He needed to focus. He needed to move quickly. He stepped back outside and relocked the office building, then worked his way through the auction area, around the canteen, up and down the rows of vendor booths. His shirt was sticking to his chest and his shoes made a squeaky sound with every step.

Maybe Josh was back at the buggy.

Maybe he was waiting for him there.

But only Beauty looked up when he ran back to where he was parked. No Josh in the front seat. No Josh in the back seat or on the floorboard. Zeb swiped at the rain and tears that were dripping down his face. He perched on the edge of the seat, buggy door open, looking out at the darkness that was settling over everything.

He couldn't do this.

He simply could not do this anymore. He was a terrible parent. Josh's disappearance proved what he'd feared all along. He could not be trusted to raise a child on his own. He wanted to give in to the feeling of worthlessness that threatened to overwhelm his soul.

And that was when he heard Ezekiel's words. Gotte *has chosen you.*

He pulled in a deep breath. *It's a precious job.*

Sat up straighter. Gotte *will also equip you.*

Squared his shoulders. And suddenly he heard not the

bishop, but his own son as he'd put him to bed two or three nights ago. Josh had put his arms around Zeb's neck and squeezed tightly, then said, "I love you, *Dat*."

He'd been tired—more tired than usual. He'd been ready to go to the living room, enjoy a cup of tea, write in his journal. He'd been tired and impatient. Had he even hugged him back? Had he told his son how much he loved him? Zeb would give all he owned to relive that moment, to feel his son's arms around him, to hear his sweet voice. Josh did love him, and Zeb loved Josh. He was a good *dat*. Not a perfect *dat*. Who was? But a good *dat*. His son was simply young.

Young children sometimes ran away.

The question now was how was he going to find him?

And suddenly he knew what to do. He knew that he couldn't do this alone, and that he'd been foolish to ever think that he could. Family and friends and people from church and people he worked with, they would all be willing to help. They'd offered many times and in so many way.

Zeb hopped out of the buggy, spoke again to the mare, then strode back toward the office.

It was time he learned to ask for help when he needed it.

This wasn't something he needed to do alone. It probably was something he couldn't do alone. After all, he couldn't be in one place looking and still be at the buggy in case his son came back. He needed help. And he was ready and willing to ask for it.

Eunice nearly dropped the plate she was drying on the floor when her *dat*'s phone rang. Her *dat*'s phone never rang. The only reason he had one was because of the market. The bishop usually approved cell phones for business owners, but many people kept theirs turned off and in the barn. Her *dat* kept his on the counter in case anyone at the market needed him. But the market was closed. Who could possibly be calling?

"Wrong number, maybe," Amos muttered as he picked up the phone, peered at it suspiciously, then flipped it open.

"*Ya*, this is Amos. Okay. Slow down. Okay. We'll be right there. Yes. Meet us in the parking area." He flipped the phone shut, stuffed it into his pocket, then turned to Eunice. "Josh is missing. He's probably somewhere on the market grounds. Zeb needs our help."

She had a thousand questions. And she didn't ask a single one. Instead, she rushed to her room, grabbed her purse off the hook by the door, then snatched up her coat. By the time she made it to the front porch, she could see her father in the barn, harnessing Oreo.

Eunice ran to Becca's house, clamored up the steps and burst through the front door.

She'd been to her *schweschder*'s house many times.

But what she saw there in that unscripted moment was so simple and touching that it brought tears to her eyes even as her heart was thudding away in fear for Josh. Becca sat in a rocker, knitting something with a soft yellow yarn—probably for Sarah's baby. Little Mary lay on the floor, her chin propped in her hand, a picture book open in front of her. And Gideon was lying on the couch, Abram sound asleep on his chest.

"What's wrong?" Becca asked.

"It's Josh. He's missing. Zeb is at the market, and he needs our help. He needs help looking."

By the time she got those few words out, Gideon was already up, handing Abram over to Becca and fetching his hat and coat. He hurried out the front door, no doubt to help her *dat* with the horse.

"We'll pray," Becca said. "He'll be okay, Eunice."

"Okay. Right." She nodded, wanting to believe it, needing to believe it.

"Please let him be alright," she whispered as she ran to catch up with Gideon.

She climbed into the back of the buggy, and her *dat* passed her the phone.

"The numbers for the phone booths are programmed in. Call and leave messages."

Her fingers were shaking as she worked her way through the menu. She'd used the phone maybe once. The first time she hit End instead of Enter and the call dropped. The second time, she got through and left a message. She called the five closest phone booths, left three messages and spoke with two *youngies*. They'd get the word out. You could always count on teenagers to spread the word.

By the time she'd flipped the phone shut, they were turning into the market's parking area. She was surprised to see several buggies and a Shipshewana police cruiser parked next to Zeb's buggy.

"It was Zeb's idea to call the police," Amos said. "I thought it was best to have all the help we can get."

The officer was just finishing up when Eunice stepped out of the buggy. She heard him say that they'd get the word out. All four of the Shipshewana police officers on duty would join in the search. Eunice wanted to go to Zeb, to assure him that everything would be all right, but she held back. Maybe now wasn't the time.

Then he looked up, his gaze locked on hers and she couldn't stop herself. She dashed across the space between them and threw herself into his arms. "It'll be okay," she promised.

"I know it will. I'm so glad you came." Zeb hugged her tightly, then stepped back. "Amos, Gideon. *Danki* for coming."

"Tell me how we can help," Amos said.

And even as Zeb explained where the police were looking and who was coordinating search teams, more buggies
pulled into the area. Eunice wasn't surprised. Amish helped
one another. They showed up in a crisis. But then she saw
Old Tom's large SUV, and Jocelyn's van and finally Martin's
retrofitted school bus. And she understood in that moment
that they weren't merely an Amish community. They were
more than that. They were a small town made up of Amish
and *Englisch* that cared for one another, looked out for one
another, and helped when they could.

Each person stopped to encourage Zeb, who now had
his *bruder* standing beside him. Samuel looked concerned.
Well, of course he was concerned. How was it that she'd
never thought of him as an adult? He'd simply clung to his
rumspringa a bit longer than most. Or perhaps he hadn't
met the right woman yet. Possibly he would live a happy
and productive life as a single person. It wasn't unheard of
in an Amish community.

Gideon had retrieved a box of flashlights, which he proceeded to pass out. The *Englischers* were using their phones
to light their way. The Amish accepted the flashlights. Eunice reached into the box, retrieved one, flipped the switch
to On. A small oval of light projected onto the path, and she
let it lead her away from the parking area.

Several of the *youngies* were setting up a coffee stand. The
rain had stopped, but even as the skies cleared, the night grew
colder. Gideon had turned on most of the ground lighting,
which they only used at Christmas when they had markets
in the evening. It provided a soft light along the footpaths.
Eunice thought it was possible that Josh would look out from
wherever he was, see the lights and follow them. Or maybe
he would see beams from the phones and flashlights. From
a distance, they must look like dozens of lightning bugs.

Eunice was headed toward the center of the market. She stopped and turned to look back at Zeb. He was showing a small sheet of paper to Amos. Eunice wanted to read the note. She understood that it was what he'd found in the seat of the buggy. It was what Josh had written. She'd heard the police officer talking about it. They weren't worried about an abduction, only about a small child who'd picked a cold night to run away. Her curiosity could wait. The important thing now was to find Josh.

Searchers were broadening out from the market, checking adjacent stores and restaurants.

Have you seen a small Amish boy?

Nein. *We don't have a picture, but he's about this tall.*

Dark pants, blue shirt, suspenders. Dark coat. He might have been wearing a straw hat.

If you think of anything, please phone the police.

As Eunice walked the perimeter of the market, she heard her friends approaching strangers, saying the same things over and over. She kept walking. Josh loved the market. He'd told her once that it seemed like an Amish Disneyland. He hadn't been to Disneyland, but he'd seen a poster for it.

"Would you like to go?" she'd asked. "To Disneyland?"

"*Nein.* Not now. Maybe when I'm older. Like seven."

Eunice had accepted her feelings for Zeb. She loved him whether he was ready to love again or not. She cared for him and believed she always would. But as she walked the perimeter of the market, as little snippets of past conversations with Josh played in her mind, she realized that sometime in the last few months, she'd also learned to love this little boy.

He wasn't merely a cute kid.

He wasn't only her best friend's boy.

He was Joshua Mast, a very special young person. And he always would be, regardless of what happened between her and Zeb. Eunice had never felt much of a maternal urge. Not when she held her nieces or nephews. Not when she helped with the *bopplin* during church luncheons. Not when she couldn't sleep at night and lay staring at the ceiling wondering about her future. But she felt that maternal pull now.

Her heart ached.

Her throat tightened.

Her mind wanted to lurch about.

So she stopped, closed her eyes, prayed for wisdom and clarity. Then she started walking again. She was now on the opposite side of the market, probably directly across from the parking area where Zeb was waiting for his son. She looked around, seeing only the dim outline of the auction barn, the canteen, the office building and vendor stalls.

The Backyard Barnyard.

Her mind flashed back on how excited Josh had been that October day when she'd watched him while working at the Barnyard. The day he'd fallen off the cow. The day Zeb had decided he couldn't trust her with his child. That was behind them now—at least she thought it was.

Eunice climbed over the three-slat wooden fence, which was mostly for appearance, and began to walk toward the barn. Her shoes squished in the wet grass. Her dress clung to her body. Her *kapp* felt like a damp rag. She played the flashlight's beam along the ground as she jogged the last few steps.

Looking down she saw that someone had already been there. Large footprints told her someone had come from the opposite direction and gone inside. She wasn't the first to think to look here. And still—

She opened the door of the barn, shone the flashlight over the small ticket office, the supply area, then proceeded back toward the animal pens. The weather report had been predicting rain all day, and whomever had closed up the Barnyard had secured the animals inside for the evening.

The ponies nodded their heads, eyes wide, no doubt wondering why she was stumbling around in the dark.

The goats bleated, sounding for all the world like a child.

The rabbits hopped when her beam fell on them, noses twitching, eyes dark and solemn.

The milk cow swung her big head toward Eunice and mooed softly.

Finally, she came to the sheep area. At first it looked like all the other pens. The sheep had bedded down, so the beam of her flashlight only revealed a pile of wool—tan, white, gray, brown and blue.

Blue.

Her heart leaped as if she'd received a jolt of revelation and maybe she had. She opened the pen, hurried over to the boy, stepped through and around the sheep who began baaing loudly. Loud enough to wake up a five-year-old boy.

Josh rubbed at his eyes as he sat up.

Eunice dropped down beside him and pulled the child into her arms.

"Hey, Eunice."

"Hey, Josh."

They stayed that way a moment—Eunice offering a silent prayer of gratitude, Josh patting her back with his small hand. She must have been holding him tightly, because he began to squirm. He pulled away from her, cocked his head and said, "Say, Eunice. What are you doing here?"

"We were looking for you, Josh."

Now his expression changed—in the blink of an eye he went from mildly curious to terribly sad. "If you mean my *dat*, he doesn't really want to find me."

"That's not true, Josh."

"It is." He sighed heavily. "I'm nothing but a bother."

It occurred to Eunice that she should run outside, shout at the top of her lungs, let everyone know that the child who was lost had been found. But she thought that perhaps that could wait another minute. Maybe what she was doing right this second was more important. So she sat on the ground that was covered with hay, sat with her back pressed against the wall of the pen and patted the spot beside her.

Josh shrugged and moved so that he was sitting next to her. Their legs splayed out in front of them, his much shorter than hers. She turned the beam of the flashlight toward the far wall so that it provided a small bit of light for them.

"Why do you think you're a bother?"

"Stick around and you'll see. I'm always doing stuff wrong. I'm always making him mad."

"Mad?" She asked the question gently.

"Okay, maybe not mad. But frustrated, you know? Like when I track in mud, or get my clothes dirty or drop something and it breaks. He goes like this." He dropped his shoulders dramatically and let out a massive sigh. "See?"

"*Ya*. I do."

"Why are you smiling?"

"Because I remember my *dat* and my oldest *schweschder* having the same reaction to me."

"They did?"

"Yup. You know, Josh. My *mamm* passed when I was only four years old."

"I was three." His voice trembled and he pulled in his bottom lip.

"I know you were. It's hard to lose a *mamm* when you're so young."

Josh nodded, swiping at his eyes with his sleeve.

"But it was just as hard on my *schweschdern*, and they were older. No matter our age, we miss people when they pass."

"I miss *Mamm* something awful."

"Of course you do and so does your *dat*."

"Is that why he's so grumpy?"

"Maybe." She shrugged because honestly she didn't know how to answer that question. "We just have to give people time, let *Gotte* do the healing in their heart."

"I guess." Then he said what he'd been holding back. "Some days I'm afraid I'll forget what she looked like."

"Josh, look at me." When he did, she turned toward him so that they were looking directly at each other. She reached forward and put her hand against his shirt, against his heart. "Your *mamm* is here, in your heart, Joshua. You might sometimes forget the color of her eyes or the way her hair fell on her shoulders, but you'll never forget her. Your heart won't let that happen."

"Okay." His voice was small—hoping, trusting.

Eunice waited another beat, then stood, brushed off her dress and held a hand out to Josh. He looked at her, searched her face for something, then gave her an impish grin that she would remember if she lived to be older than the oldest member of their congregation. She would see that tender smile in her dreams.

"Guess we should go find *Dat*." He put his hand in hers.

"Guess we should."

"He's going to be awfully mad."

"Maybe not. He just might surprise you."

They walked across the grass, walked toward the center of the lights where Zeb was waiting. When he saw them, for a moment he froze, almost as if he was afraid to believe his eyes. And then he ran toward them, wrapped his arms around them both and held them close.

Chapter Sixteen

The next two weeks passed in a blur. Each night Zeb woke from a nightmare—a terrible dream in which once again he'd lost his son. Sometimes Josh was hiding in the market. Other times he'd made it out to the highway. Occasionally he was lying in a creek bed. Each time, Zeb lurched from bed shaking and feeling ill. Each time, he calmed his breathing, told himself it was only a dream, then walked down the hall to check on his son.

He would have liked to say that after that terrible night at the market he never again lost his patience. Not true. He hadn't become a perfect father that night. But maybe he'd become a better one. Maybe he'd realized in the moment he saw Eunice and Josh walking toward him, walking hand in hand, what a blessed man he was.

He continued attending counseling sessions. He met weekly with the bishop. He wrote to Suzanne's family in Pennsylvania telling them he would be staying in Indiana. Shipshe was his home, and it was Josh's home. He would build their lives here. And he focused on making small but important changes in his relationship with his son.

No matter how busy he was, Zeb took a half hour each afternoon to play with his son—whether it was throwing a ball back and forth, playing hide-and-seek in the yard or checkers on the front porch. And every evening, he set aside his worries and spent an hour helping his son ready for bed, talking to him about his day, hearing his worries and also the things that had made him laugh.

They'd begun going to the Shipshewana library and checking out books—simple ones to be sure, but ones that Josh was interested in studying.

Did Zeb know that sheep had long wooly tails that kept them warm?

Pigs make their bed every day.

Hens make friends.

Cows love music.

His son's interest in animals seemed to know no limits. It was Eunice who came up with the idea to visit the petting farm over in Middlebury, which they did the last Saturday in January. Samuel had taken over the tours for the day, and Becca had assured them she could be the fourth stop. She'd spend a half hour telling them about her mission trips. Zeb realized he should take off one Saturday a month to spend with his family. Work wasn't that important, and people were more than willing to help.

He and Eunice hadn't begun dating again, but they were intentional about spending time together with Josh. To try and support the boy as a pair.

The day dawned cold but beautiful.

Josh could barely eat his breakfast he was so excited, and he readily moved to the back seat when they picked up Eunice.

"Gosh, you look pretty today, Eunice."

"Stole the words right out of my mouth, son."

Eunice blushed a soft pink, then changed the subject to the lunch she'd packed for them.

There were a dozen things that Zeb could and probably

needed to do that day. They'd decided not to have tours during the month of February since the weather tended toward unpredictable. The tours had been a success though. Zeb and Samuel had gone to the bank the previous week and finalized the paperwork to purchase the farm. Zeb was thrilled about that and also aware that he needed to rise to the occasion. Instead of going to a petting zoo, he needed to tend to things in his own barn, clean the house, wash sheets, scrub the kitchen.

He didn't do those things though. He didn't even mention them as the three of them walked through the Critter Cove Farm. He held Eunice's hand and watched his son delight in the animals which included sheep, rabbits, goats, chickens, ducks and swans, ponies, alpacas, pigs and a miniature donkey no larger than a dog.

With each new animal encountered, Josh turn to his father and say, "Wouldn't it be great to have one of these at home?"

Zeb would smile, nod and pray fervently that his son forgot that particular wish before his birthday.

"It's his third time to visit the sheep," Eunice pointed out. "Maybe you should get some."

"*Ya*. Another chore is exactly what I need." But he laughed when he said it. He heard the joy in his laughter, and he thought maybe Eunice heard it too because she smiled up at him and squeezed his hand.

"He seems better, *ya*?"

"I think so. I think the fact that I've been spending more time with him has helped."

"And maybe it was simply something he had to go through. Part of his journey."

Zeb nodded. Her words reflected exactly what he'd been thinking.

The owners of the petting farm had furnished a small,

older barn with picnic tables, installed large gas heaters and offered free coffee, tea or hot chocolate. Eunice's meal included thick slices of ham, fresh bread, potato salad and cookies.

"You're a *gut* cook, Eunice."

"*Danki*, Josh. My *schweschder* Becca is teaching me."

Josh found that awfully funny. "You're going to cooking school?"

"I suppose I am."

"Don't get in trouble, Eunice. Or you'll have to clean the chalkboard." Laughter spilled from him and he reached over to high-five Zeb.

In customary Josh-like fashion, the boy gulped down his sandwich and two forks full of the potato salad, then asked if he could go and play in the small playground area set up in a corner of the barn.

"Yes, son, but—"

"Be careful. Got it." Josh dashed off.

Eunice started laughing.

"What's so funny?" Zeb tried to sound offended, but he couldn't quite pull it off.

"He was running like that when I first saw him, and the first day you brought him to stay with me. That boy loves to run."

"He might grow up to be a professional runner."

"And a sheep farmer."

"He could do both."

"Indeed, he could." Eunice's eyes were still on Josh, when she said softly, "I love him, you know."

"*Ya.* He cares for you too. We both care for you, Eunice."

She pulled her eyes from the children playing a rousing game of tag, and turned to study Zeb.

He struggled to swallow.

Took a drink of the coffee, which didn't help at all.

His hands started to sweat. He knew what he was about to do, and he couldn't believe that he was going to do it. Here. Now. He should wait until they resumed dating, but he'd already gone too many days without Eunice by his side. He wanted to change that, and he wanted to change it now.

"We both love you, Eunice."

Her eyes widened, but still she didn't say anything.

"Took me some time to accept that. I guess for a while I saw it as some kind of betrayal to Suzanne. But now I know it's not that. She would want Josh to have a *mamm*. She'd want me to be happy."

"Zeb Mast. Are you asking me to marry you in a barn?"

"Now that you mention it..." He scooted closer to her on the picnic bench, reached for both of her hands, held them in his. "*Ya*. I am. Will you marry me, Eunice? Will you be my *fraa* and Josh's *mamm*? You would make me a very happy man. And I would try with all of my being to make you a happy woman."

"I am happy because I love you both too." She leaned forward and kissed him on the cheek. "And my answer is yes."

The next few days flew. Eunice waited until Sunday morning, until her entire family was gathered together, to tell them her news.

Ada threw her arms in the air and shouted, "She's tying her *kapp* strings!" Then she jumped up and enfolded Eunice in a hug as someone muttered, "Tying the knot is what she means."

Sarah had tears in her eyes. Now that she was in the third trimester of her pregnancy, she was more emotional than ever. "Happy tears," she assured Eunice.

Each of her *schweschdern* and each of her *bruders*-in-law

gave her a hug, whispered *congratulations* and *we love you* and words of blessing. Eunice didn't realize how much she'd craved her family's blessing until they'd given it.

Her *dat* didn't even seem surprised. In fact, he nodded his head as if he'd expected as much.

"You knew, didn't you?" They were standing on the front porch, watching Zeb's buggy turn into their lane.

"Zeb came to me two weeks ago. Told me he cared for you and would like to ask you to marry him. I gave him my blessing, of course."

"Two weeks ago?"

"*Ya.* After you found Josh. I think he had several revelations that day."

"Such as?" She could see Josh waving now. She offered a small wave in return.

"How blessed he is. How much he cares for his son. How important you are to him."

Her *dat* pulled her closer to his side and kissed the top of her head. Eunice thought that it was a show of affection that she wouldn't mind receiving well into her old age.

"You'll be alone," she said. It was her one worry. The thing that had caused her to toss and turn the last few nights.

"How can I possibly be alone, Eunice? *Gotte* has blessed me with a large family, with sons and *doschdern* who live close and enjoy visiting, and with *grandkinner* that fill my heart with joy."

"Josh will be your grandson." She hadn't realized it until that moment. She had worried about her father eating by himself, puttering around a large empty house, wondering if his best days were behind him. But it hadn't occurred to her that he'd be gaining another son and a grandchild.

"Josh will be your grandson," she repeated.

"That he will be. *Gotte* is good."

"All the time," she whispered, then jogged down the steps to take the container of oatmeal bars from Josh and kiss Zeb.

The Sunday meal was a time of laughter and being genuinely thankful. She would look up from what she was doing and see one of her *schweschdern* pulling Zeb into a hug or one of her *bruders*-in-law slapping him on the back. They didn't speak of the engagement openly. Everyone had agreed to wait until she and Zeb had a private moment to speak with Josh.

In the afternoon, when the smaller children were asleep and the parents wished they were as well, Zeb asked Eunice if she'd like to go on a walk with him and Josh. They'd spoken with each other at least once a day since the visit to the petting zoo, either in person or by going to the phone booth. They'd decided that today would be the day that they'd tell Josh.

The day was cold with low clouds that looked as if they might dump several inches of snow at any moment. A light dusting lay on the ground. No wind though. Good for walking. Josh ran ahead as they walked toward the barn, through Eunice's work area, and back out the other side.

Josh spoke to each of the horses who had been let loose in the field. As soon as they'd seen the boy, they trotted over, sure that he had a treat in his pocket—and he did.

"He learned that from you, I do believe," Zeb said.

"Guilty."

Zeb reached for her hand. She loved that about him, that he showed her in so many small ways that he was thinking about her, that he cared for her. "Walking through your workroom reminded me of something."

Eunice froze like a rabbit caught in a flashlight beam. She'd been ready for Zeb to ask her to marry him that day at the zoo. She'd hoped and prayed he would. But she didn't know if she was ready for this conversation. She'd spent her entire life apologizing for her interests, trying to explain her hobbies, hoping people would understand. They rarely did.

Better that they speak of this now than after they were married, she supposed. So she turned to him, forced her eyes to meet his, and said, "And what did my workroom remind you of?"

She feared he would say something about her needing to be a traditional wife. Or that she'd have no time for playing with gadgets once she was a *fraa* and a *mamm*. But Zeb surprised her. He reached forward, tucked a strand of hair into her *kapp* and said, "I need to create a similar area in my barn for you. You'll need a place to continue your work."

"And you won't mind?"

"Mind? I'm proud of you and what you do, Eunice. I think you're amazing. And I would never want to stand in the way of that."

She melted into his arms, which of course was when Josh dashed back to where they were and announced, "Gross. Are you guys about to kiss?"

Eunice pulled away, and Zeb laughed. "We might have been about to kiss, but then we were interrupted."

"Grown-up stuff." Josh kicked the dirt floor, then looked up at the two of them, a concerned look on his face. "Anything I need to know about?"

"Actually there is," Zeb said.

"How about we sit out on the bench?" Eunice suggested. "We can watch the horses and wait for the snow as we talk."

"Are we going to talk that long? It might not snow until tomorrow or next week." Josh ducked out of the way when his *dat* reached to squeeze his neck.

They sat on the bench.

Josh in the middle.

Eunice on one side.

Zeb on the other.

Eunice waited. She thought it was Zeb's place to start this conversation. She wasn't sure if he was going to carefully work up to the topic or plunge right in.

"Son, Eunice and I love each other."

Plunge right in. Good. She liked that approach.

"*Ya,* I know." Josh said. "Ezekiel preached about it last week. We are all called to love one another."

He swung his feet, glanced at Eunice, then looked at his dad. "Oh. You mean love love. Like married love?"

He jumped off the bench and turned to face them. "Are you two getting married?"

"We are," Zeb said.

Eunice nodded her head and smiled. What could she say to this dear child? She could practically see the wheels of his brain turning, making sense of what Zeb had told him.

"So, like… You're going to be my *mamm*." His smile had slipped a little.

And she knew him so well, that she knew he was thinking of Suzanne, of his confession that he might forget who she was and what she looked like. Of his fear of losing his mother from his heart.

"Listen to me, Josh." Eunice waited until she had his complete attention. "Suzanne will always be your mother. That will never change."

"She's in heaven though."

"Exactly. She's in heaven, and she's in your heart."

"Okay. I suppose that will work. One *mamm* up there. One *mamm* here. What am I supposed to call you?"

"What do you want to call her, son?"

"I don't know. I'm only five. This is hard stuff." But the

smile was tugging at his lips again. "I guess I could call you Eunice."

"Which would be great," she assured him. "After all, it is my name."

"Are you going to live with us?"

"Yup."

"Like…now?"

Zeb laughed and shook his head. "We'll have the ceremony first. You've been to weddings, Josh. You know what they're like."

"Sure, but I never needed to pay attention before." He took off his hat, squished it into a different shape that quickly popped back into the original shape, plopped it on his head and announced, "I think it'd be nice to have this done before my birthday."

"That's only a few months away," Zeb reminded him. But then he looked at Eunice.

She knew that he saw all of her then—the hopes and dreams and yes, even the same impatience that Josh felt. She nodded.

"We'll speak to Ezekiel," Zeb said.

Which seemed to be a good enough answer for Josh. He dashed toward the pasture fence. Zeb and Eunice walked out into the cloudy day—a day filled with the possibility of snow, the likelihood of a lifetime of such talks and the probability of a growing family. Zeb pulled her close to his side, and Eunice basked in the solidness of this man—both his presence and his love.

Josh ran back, threw his arms around both of their legs at once, then dashed away again.

"I think he's okay with this," Eunice said.

"Of course, he is. He's a smart kid. He knows a good deal when he hears one."

"A good deal, huh?"

"Probably could have said that in a more romantic way."

"Oh, I love being referred to as a good deal. Makes me feel like a new buggy."

And then they were both laughing, walking back toward the house, walking in the last light of a winter day. Josh dashed past them, ran up the porch steps and into the house. They could hear him announcing to all, "Eunice is marrying my *dat*. Can you believe it?"

She would have followed Josh inside, but Zeb tugged on her hand, nodded toward a corner of the porch that afforded them a little privacy and pulled her into his arms. Eunice couldn't remember ever feeling happier.

Life was a journey, as her *dat* had said. She and Zeb and Josh were embarking on a journey together. And she couldn't wait to see what was around the bend.

Epilogue

On the afternoon of the second Tuesday in March, Eunice stood next to Zeb as Ezekiel presented them to all those assembled—which seemed to include everyone in their Amish community and a few *Englischers* to boot. Ada and Becca and Bethany had decorated the Yoder barn with fresh boughs of cedar, a couple hundred white carnations and small twinkly lights that operated off batteries. Sarah had overseen the placement of benches, tables and chairs—though no one would allow her to actually lift anything. She was only a few weeks away from delivery now, and they were all treating her with great care even though so far the pregnancy had been completely normal.

The heavy snows had come late and seemed determined to stay. Two feet of white fluffy powder lay on the ground. The market was still closed for the winter season, which worked well since most of the employees wanted to attend the wedding ceremony.

Eunice's pulse beat a bit faster than normal and her senses seemed especially sharp. The cedar boughs smelled fresh and woodsy. The lights practically sparkled. The man beside her seemed more handsome and more solid than she'd ever known him to be, and she'd known him a very long time. She had a sudden image of the two of them inside a snow globe. Only this time the snow globe was entirely composed of the important things in their life.

Ezekiel had been speaking, but Eunice had lost the thread of what he was saying. Suddenly, he cleared his throat, paused and waited for her and Zeb to turn their gaze to him. "All of those assembled here, your friends and family in Christ, and I, as your bishop, wish you the blessing and mercy of God."

Eunice and Zeb were facing each other, her hands in his, Ezekiel's hands on top of theirs. The old bishop's tender expression reminded Eunice of being a child, of sitting on her *mamm*'s lap, of being truly cared for. In the absence of her mother, she knew that Ezekiel and her *dat* and her siblings would help guide her and Zeb. She would always miss her *mamm*, especially in moments like this one. But *Gotte* had provided.

Ezekiel's smile grew, stretching the corners of his beard. With tears shining in his eyes, he turned them toward those witnessing the ceremony.

Eunice glanced up in time to see her family's reaction. Her father wiped at his eyes. Sarah reached over and clasped his hand. Ada said something that made everyone smile. Josh stood between Becca and Bethany. Oh, how she loved her family. They were, even now, pulling Josh into their circle of love.

Ezekiel cleared his throat. "Go forth in the Lord's name. You are now man and wife."

"Hal-le-lujah!" Josh shouted and tossed his hat into the air.

Which seemed to express the sentiment that everyone was feeling. Eunice couldn't believe she'd made it through the whirlwind of the last two months. Couples classes with Ezekiel. Planning meetings with the Amish caterer. Dressmaking sessions with her *schweschdern*. The pale green dress she wore would always remind her of the promise of spring and this place where she'd learned to be an adult and embrace new beginnings.

It was later, after the meal and the cake, after the guests had left and only her family—her complete family that included Ezekiel and Samuel—remained. Ada picked that moment to share what she'd said to their *dat* at the end of the ceremony.

"Told him it was his turn to fall head over suspenders for someone."

No one corrected her. No one needed to.

Instead, Sarah put a hand to her stomach and said, "She might have a point, *Dat*."

"You did it, after all," Becca said.

Bethany reached for her *doschder*'s hand. "You matched all your girls to *wunderbaar* men."

"I'm not sure I was that involved," Amos said with a twinkle in his eye.

Sarah and Becca and Bethany and Eunice and Ada all shared a look. Then they broke into laughter.

The men had been loading benches into the bench trailer which had been pulled inside the barn. At the sound of laughter, they looked up to see what they'd missed, but it was Josh, who dashed over, straw stuck to his hat, icing from the wedding cake smeared across one cheek, and said, "This family sure is growing. All we need now is a *grossmammi*."

Then he high-fived his *grossdaddi*, said something to Lydia and they both dashed off to play with Mary.

"Out of the mouths of babes," Ezekiel murmured.

Eunice didn't know if her *dat* would ever marry again. As far as she was aware, he'd never been interested in another woman since her *mamm* had died. He'd built his entire life around his church and the market and his family. She couldn't imagine him slowing down long enough to court someone.

But then Eunice knew better than anyone that you could not predict what might happen next in a person's life.

Zeb helped her up into his buggy. Some of the *young-ies* had chalked "Just Hitched" across the back and paper streamers of green and white and silver had been tied to every possible surface.

Josh stood with her family on the front porch, waving, as she and Zeb drove down the lane. Samuel and Joshua would stay in Eunice's old room. Eunice and Zeb would spend their wedding night alone at their home and return in the morning to pick up their son. A proper honeymoon would wait until spring had officially arrived.

Eunice didn't mind.

She was married to the man of her dreams, though she hadn't known it when he'd shown up at her barn with an old solar pump that needed fixing. She certainly hadn't known it when they'd been friends in school.

She knew it now though.

Her heart knew that they were meant to be together—the three of them.

Eunice thought it was shaping up to be the best year of her life. The best of everything. As her father often said, "*Gotte* is good." To which her heart replied, "All the time."

* * * * *

Dear Reader,

Sometimes the future we envision isn't nearly as grand as what God has planned.

Eunice Yoder is not your conventional Amish woman. She's accepted that about herself, but she doesn't expect to ever find a man who is willing to accept it as well—to love her in spite of her eccentric ways. Then Zebedee Mast and his young son, Joshua, walk into her life.

Zeb is still grieving the loss of his wife. It's been two years, and he doesn't feel one bit better than the day he was widowed. In some ways, he even blames himself and perhaps that is what keeps him from moving forward. But God has plans for both Eunice, Zeb and young Josh. This is a story of being wounded, finding healing and embracing a future beyond one's wildest dreams.

I hope you enjoyed reading *A Courtship for the Amish Spinster*. I welcome comments and letters at vannettachapman@gmail.com.

May we continue "giving thanks always for all things unto God the Father in the name of our Lord Jesus Christ" (Ephesians 5:20).

Blessings,
Vannetta